SUMMIT OF DESIRE

The Springs—Seven

ELENA AITKEN

Also by Elena Aitken

The Springs Series

Summer of Change

Falling Into Forever

Second Glances

Winter's Burn

Midnight Springs

She's Making A List

Summit of Desire

Summit of Seduction

Summit of Passion

Fighting For Forever

The Springs Collection: Volume 1

The Springs Collection: Volume 2

The Springs Collection: Volume 3

The Springs Complete Collection - Books 1-10

The McCormicks

Love in the Moment

Only for a Moment

One more Moment

In this Moment

From this Moment

Our Perfect Moment

Destination Paradise

Shelter by the Sea

Escape to the Sun

Hidden in the Sand

Ever After

Choosing Happily Ever After

Needing Happily Ever After

Wanting Happily Ever After

Fighting Happily Ever After

We Wish You A Happily Ever After

Keeping Happily Ever After

Finding Happily Ever After

Seeking Happily Ever After

Cherishing Happily Ever After

Ever After: Volume One (Books 1-4)

Stand Alone Stories

All We Never Knew

Drawing Free

Sugar Crash

Composing Myself

Betty & Veronica

The Escape Collection

Vegas

Nothing Stays in Vegas

Return to Vegas

His to Tame

His to Seek

Hers for the Season

Bears of Grizzly Ridge: Books 1-4

Bears of Grizzly Ridge: Books 5-8

Halfway Series

Halfway to Nowhere

Halfway in Between

Halfway to Christmas

Chapter One

AS SHE RODE up the chairlift, Kylie Wilson took a minute to take in the view. In front of her, dozens of ski runs snaked through the pine trees and a smattering of people carved their way down the slopes in perfect *S* formations. With a clear blue sky overhead, they couldn't have asked for a more perfect day for skiing. Especially considering it was the official opening week of Stone Summit, her boyfriend, Malcolm Stones's, ski resort. He'd been working tirelessly for months to make the re-opening of the hill a success, but the one thing they hadn't been able to control was the weather. Fortunately, Mother Nature had been very cooperative and had provided an abundance of white fluffy snow on the ski hill that was just up from the town of Cedar Springs.

"I can't believe it's finally happening, and we'll be officially open after tonight."

Kylie turned to look at Malcolm next to her on the chairlift. Even in his ski jacket and helmet, with goggles covering half his face, he was incredibly handsome. She smiled and leaned over to kiss him.

"It's great," she said. "And it looks like everyone's having fun."

It was true. The occasional strains of laughter floated up from the runs below to reach them on the chairlift. The town had been looking forward to the re-opening of the hill because for the people who lived in a mountain town, there was nothing more fun than spending weekends on the slopes. It had been sorely missed. To get everyone even more excited, in the week since Christmas, they'd had a "soft opening" where the townspeople of Cedar Springs had exclusive access to the ski hill. It had actually been Kylie's idea. She'd suggested that in order to be successful, they'd need to have everyone in town on board, and the best way to do that was to make them a part of the experience.

So far, it had worked perfectly.

"Are you having a good time?"

Kylie nodded but glanced away so he couldn't see her face. "I am." She wanted to add that she was having fun now that they were on the chairlift, far away from all the chaos that was taking place in the offices down below. Sitting on the chairlift with Malcolm was the first time she'd been alone with her boyfriend in weeks; except for a few stolen moments on Christmas Day, he'd been working nonstop and sure, she understood that opening an entire ski hill took work, but still. She missed him. A lot.

"I'm glad we're doing this," Kylie added, referring to the fact that they were going to take their opening day ski together. And it almost hadn't happened, as Malcolm came up with a million reasons why he couldn't get away and if she hadn't insisted, there was no doubt in her mind he'd still be in his office, working away on one thing or another. But the ski had been his idea. After all, they'd originally met at that very same ski hill many years before.

Of course, things had turned out differently back then.

Kylie had ended up dating Malcolm's twin brother, Marcus, and it wasn't until a year ago when Malcolm surprised her with a secretive invitation to an exclusive tropical island that he declared his love for her, and Kylie realized it had always been Malcolm in her heart.

It was the type of happy-ever-after ending fairytales were made of, which is why everything should have been perfect between them. Should have. Kylie's smile dimmed as she thought about all the times over the last few months that she'd questioned herself and even more troubling, when she'd questioned their relationship. But she wasn't going to think about that now. Not when she was finally spending that time with Malcolm and they were together and happy. No. She shook her head hard. There was no time for those doubts now.

"I'm glad, too." Malcolm put his gloved hand over hers and squeezed. "Are you ready?"

She nodded and he lifted the safety bar as their chair approached the top of the hill and the end of the lift. Easily they each skied off and onto the ridge under the Stone Summit trail marker sign.

"Let me take your picture." Kylie sidestepped on her skis so she was in position and pulled her cellphone out of her pocket. She ignored all the text messages that had popped up on her screen. No doubt there were a ton of questions about the grand opening, New Year's Eve party that night, but they could wait for a few minutes. "Smile."

Malcolm was posed next to the sign that bore his name. She pushed the button to capture the picture. "Perfect."

"Kylie, get in here and take one with me."

"No." She shook her head. "This is your day, Malcolm. Your hill." She skied over to him.

"You're being ridiculous." He grabbed her and awkwardly pulled her toward him as much as he could with them both wearing skis. "Come on. You don't even want to take a selfie?"

She laughed, because Malcolm hated selfies and always made fun of her for taking them. He thought they were self-indulgent and silly. "Really? You want a selfie?"

"No." He took the phone from her and held it out in front of them. "But I want a picture with my girl. So come on."

She couldn't help herself; she giggled and tucked her head in next to his so he could take the shot. When he had finished, he handed back the phone and tugged his gloves back on.

"Are you ready for this?"

He looked so handsome in his ski jacket and pants. An athlete, in his element. In that moment, with both of them together, laughing, doing what they loved to do together, all of the building worries Kylie had been having melted away. It was perfect. "Let's do it."

Malcolm snapped his goggles into place. "Good, because I should get back. My phone is blowing up in my pocket." He turned and pushed off with his poles to head down the slope. And just like that, Kylie's good mood evaporated.

You're being ridiculous, she told herself. *He's just busy with this right now; it'll calm down again. Things will be back to normal again soon.* But even as she told herself that, she knew it wasn't true. Because Malcolm Stone was the type of man who was important. He made decisions, ran businesses, and created his own success. Kylie Wilson was the type of woman who still didn't know what she wanted to do with her life, and even if she did, she was too scared to do it. For God's sake, she was twenty-five and still waitressing in the Grizzly Paw pub. A successful businessman and a waitress. It wasn't the first time she'd struggled with the paradox of their relationship.

"Kylie," Malcolm called to her from a little way down the run. "Are you coming?"

No time to worry about it now anyway. She tugged her goggles on and with a strong push, skied down the hill, catching up to him in no time. If there was one thing they were equal at, it was skiing skills. And even if it wasn't much—it was something.

TAKING time out to ski with Kylie had set him back, too far back. There was way too much to do before the party that would officially signify the re-opening of Stone Summit. Malcolm had been working too hard for too long to not see the grand opening through to a final and excellent completion. It was true that the runs had been open for the last week, but it would be official after tonight, and he needed everyone, especially the competing hills in nearby towns, to know that this time Stone Summit was around for the long haul.

They left their skis propped up outside the offices, which were housed in a log building next to the main ski lodge where the cafeteria and lounge were. There were some days that Malcolm wished he would have put his offices in the lounge. It would have been easier to handle the stress if he had closer proximity to a beer now and then, but it was probably for the best that they were in a separate building.

Kylie came in with him. She pulled her helmet off and shook her dark hair out so it fell over her shoulders. God, but she was beautiful, and with her cheeks pink from the cold air outside, she looked even more perfect. His little ski bunny. Spontaneously, he pulled her into his arms and kissed her.

"Thank you," he said when he pulled away.

She laughed a little and blushed. "For what? A kiss? You know I can handle that."

"No. But that was nice, too." He brushed a strand of hair off her forehead. "For going skiing with me. The weather was perfect and the snow, and—"

"It was just nice spending time with you." She stared

straight into his eyes, challenging him. "You've been so busy lately, I feel like I haven't seen you in ages."

"I know." Guilt flashed through him, but also a flicker of annoyance. Of course he'd been busy; he was trying to open a major ski resort, practically single-handedly. Did she not get that? If he was a little busier than normal, that was to be expected. Malcolm took a breath before saying anything else. It wouldn't do anyone any good if they had an argument today. "Things will calm down again."

She nodded, but for some reason, Malcolm didn't believe that she was really okay with it.

"But for now, we're just going to have to make the best of it, okay?" He tilted her chin up so she looked straight into his eyes. "And tonight we'll ring in the New Year, okay?"

"It's going to be a crazy party, Malcolm." She shook her head gently. "There'll be people everywhere and you're going to have to—"

"Hey." She stopped and stared at him again. "It doesn't matter. Whatever craziness is going on, at the countdown, find me, okay? I want you by my side when the ball drops. I want yours to be the first face I see in the New Year and your lips to be the very first I kiss."

She opened her mouth to object, and he laughed. "And the only lips I ever kiss," he finished. She gave him a look, but he knew she wasn't angry. "Promise me we'll ring in the New Year together."

"Of course." He kissed her again, softly until she responded to him and he deepened the kiss, enjoying a thorough exploration of her mouth. One that was long overdue.

"I'd tell you to get a room, but I don't think there are any available."

Malcolm pulled away, somewhat reluctantly, to see Sandra in the doorway to the reception area. She held a stack of files, and had a smirk on her face.

"Sorry, Sandra." Kylie slipped out of his grasp. "I was just saying goodbye."

"Sure you were." The older woman tsked, but there was laughter in her eyes, and Malcolm knew her well enough after working with her for almost the last year that she wasn't in any way offended by their display of affection. In fact, knowing Sandra, she was probably happy to see the couple spending time together. She kept telling Malcolm he was working too much, and even though he knew it was true, there wasn't any other option. Not if he wanted the resort to be successful. And he did. It had to be.

Malcolm turned to face Kylie, who'd moved back toward the door. "You're leaving? I was hoping you'd be able to help the serving staff for tonight. I'm not sure they're going to be okay with all the appetizers Jax has prepared, and I want to make sure they know what to hand out when, and how to circulate the room and—"

"I'm sure you don't need Kylie to do that." Sandra rushed into the room, dropped the folders on the desk and stood between himself and Kylie. "After all, Kylie is probably—"

"No." Kylie put her hand on Sandra's arm. Was it his imagination, or did she look upset? It had to be his imagination; just a moment ago she was melting in his arms, and...no. It was nothing. "It's fine," Kylie said. "I'm sure I could help them with a few tips or something."

"If you could, that would be great." His cellphone rang and the moment he answered it and heard the voice of Seth McBride, his general manager, on the line, all worries about Kylie evaporated. He had way more pressing issues to deal with. He turned to walk into his office so he could hear the latest report on the hill's conditions, but before he did, he put his hand over the phone and turned back to Kylie. "So you'll pop in and deal with the serving staff for me?"

She nodded, but she wasn't smiling. "I'll handle it."

"Thanks, babe. You're the best. I'll see you later, okay?"

He didn't wait for an answer, but headed to his desk to cross items off his list.

LOGICALLY, Kylie knew that whatever it was going on with Malcolm would pass. And really, she knew what it was. He was busy. Really busy. After all, he was an important businessman launching a ski resort. It was huge, really, and she was just being petty, feeling upset because he wasn't being as attentive to her as she would like. She hated herself for letting it bother her, but it did.

After leaving Stone Summit, she'd gone back to her apartment to quickly change clothes and then head over the Grizzly Paw. She'd promised Samantha she'd work her shift despite the business of the day. Sam had told her not to worry about it, considering she was supposed to be helping Malcolm with the grand opening, but there was something normalizing about working in the pub. It was who she was. Even when she pretended to be a bigger deal than she was as Malcolm's significant other, it was just that—pretending.

It only took her a few minutes to walk down the main street of Cedar Springs from her small basement suite apartment to the Grizzly Paw that sat at the end of the street, next to the frozen lake. Malcolm had tried to get her to move in with him, claiming he had a lot more room in his chalet-style house that had been built along with a few other executive homes on the ski hill, but she'd been resisting. Sure, his house was beautiful, and it made sense to live together because they spent so much free time together, but she couldn't seem to let go of her little apartment. The excuse she used was that it was easy for her to get to and from work, especially when she closed the pub. It was often too late to get in her car and drive the short distance up the mountain, especially if the weather was bad.

Six months ago, she would have made the move in a heart-beat, but things had changed between them. It was subtle at first, but the more time that went on, and the busier Malcolm got, the more Kylie realized they were from different worlds. After all, he was a successful business owner. Wealthy and powerful, and she was…a waitress in a bar. And wasn't that really the problem? She wasn't good enough for him.

The feeling weighed on her the way it had been doing more and more, and she tried to shrug it off as she walked up the steps to the Paw. Before she opened the door, she took a moment to watch the ice skaters on the lake. It was one of her favorite things to do in the winter, and besides the Christmas festival, she hadn't had a moment to get out there and skate. Maybe she could drag Malcolm out tomorrow, for the annual New Year's Day party. It was a pretty low-key event, but usually her friends would gather and go skating and drink hot chocolate and just have a little fun as a way to celebrate the new year.

But she knew it wouldn't happen. Malcolm would be way too busy to get away and she'd probably spend the day waiting for him to have time to get away. Maybe she'd just have to go on her own? With a sigh, she opened the door and stepped into the busy pub.

"Hey Kylie." Archer greeted her from the bar, where he was pulling pints. Even though it was Samantha's bar, Archer was the fixture behind the bar at the Paw or in the kitchen, cooking up his famous chili. "You know you didn't have to come in today. It's going to be slow what with the big party and all."

Kylie nodded and stripped off her heavy jacket. "I know, but honestly? I wanted to come in." Archer gave her a ques-tioning look but she ignored it and went into the kitchen to hang up her jacket and put her purse away. She took an extra moment before she returned to the bar, hoping Archer would forget about the question he was obviously dying to ask.

"You going to tell me why you're not up at the Summit?"

No such luck.

Kylie sighed. "I will be later."

"And now?"

"When did you get so nosy?" It wasn't like Archer to ask so many questions. That was Sam's job. Archer usually kept his head down and made silent observations, but he rarely shared them. Not unless he thought it was really important.

"Not nosy," he said with a shrug. "Just wondering."

Kylie ignored him and tied her apron around her waist. She grabbed a tray ready to go take an order, but stopped when she realized there was only one table and Archer was setting those beers on a tray.

"I told you it would be slow today." He grinned and went to deliver the drinks.

It was slow, and she knew it would be. Everyone in town was getting ready for the party up at the Summit later. Even Cynthia Giles, her best friend, who ran the general store, had closed down early to get ready. She'd tried to convince Kylie to take off with her and get her hair done at Shear Thing, but Kylie just wasn't in to it. And what was worse, she felt guilty about it. She should be excited about the party; after all, it was Malcolm's big day and she loved Malcolm. She dropped her head in her hands on the bar and rubbed at her temples.

She was being ridiculous. Just because her boyfriend was successful didn't make her a failure. She needed to remember that. And he'd never once made her feel like she wasn't good enough. That was all her.

"You okay?"

Kylie's head shot up and she ran a hand through her hair

in an effort to pull herself together. "Of course. Why would you ask?"

Archer smirked. "Only because it's New Year's Eve. You should be getting ready for the biggest party of the year—one your boyfriend happens to be the guest of honor at—and you look like your dog just died."

"He did." Unwanted and totally unpredictable tears pricked at her eyelids. She hadn't cried about Ranger, her old German Shepard in months. And Archer knew it. He raised an eyebrow at her. "Okay, it's not Ranger I'm upset about."

"I know."

"It's just that…" The truth was she couldn't put a finger on why exactly she was upset. She had everything to be excited about, and nothing to cry about. Except the slight detail that the more successful Malcolm got, the more she felt she didn't deserve him.

"Hey." Archer held up his hand. "You certainly don't have to talk if you don't want to. In fact, I've had almost enough female emotional stuff in the last few weeks to last me awhile."

Kylie smiled; she knew he was referring to Samantha and Trent's recent wedding at Castle Mountain Lodge. Sam had been feeling the sting of all her friends moving on while she was being left behind, and she hadn't been shy in venting to her best friends, Archer included. Trent had surprised Sam with the ceremony and as the closest thing to family that Sam had, Archer had actually walked her down the aisle. No doubt he was relieved to have a little peace as far as Sam was concerned.

"Don't worry, Arch. I won't start crying on your shoulder or anything. Quite honestly, everything's fine."

He gave her a look that let her know that he was fully aware that she was lying, but Kylie also knew that he was smart enough to leave it alone. And for that, she was grateful.

"Well, if you want to talk…"

"Thanks."

Kylie forced a weak smile and got to work, washing tables and wrapping cutlery. There really wasn't much to do and it only took an hour for the last of the customers to leave. Everyone in town was getting ready for the party. Guilt crept in because that was exactly what Kylie should have been doing, too. Malcolm had ordered her a gorgeous dress to wear. Not that he needed to; she had plenty of things in her closet. Okay, she didn't. But she didn't need her boyfriend buying her outfits. It was becoming a trend and Kylie didn't like to feel like a kept lady. She didn't need someone to buy her things and take care of her, and more and more that was what Malcolm was doing. It irked her. More than irked her. It pissed her off.

"Time to go," Archer called from behind the bar and interrupted her thoughts, which was probably a good thing.

"It's not closing time." She grabbed up the rag she'd been using and joined him at the bar. "We're still open for another hour."

"You have noticed that you and I are the only ones here, right? It's time to go, Kylie." He took the rag out of her hand and tossed it into the sink before he squeezed her shoulder gently. "Come on. Let's go to your boyfriend's party."

She had to swallow a groan, which only made her feel guiltier.

"And smile, Kylie. It's a party. It's supposed to be fun."

Chapter Two

BY THE TIME Kylie had a quick shower and blew out her hair, she'd managed to shake her mood. Archer was right; it was a party and it would be fun. There was so much to celebrate tonight: a new year, a new ski hill, a new start. There was no reason for her to feel inadequate about being with Malcolm. That stuff was all in her head and she needed to push it out. The hot water had helped, as had the glass of red she sipped while she applied her makeup. Cynthia was picking her up because Malcolm knew he wouldn't be able to get away to come get her. She'd spend the night with Malcolm in his chalet.

Cynthia was right on time, which actually surprised her, because Cynthia was never on time. She looked amazing in a silver dress that set off her red hair perfectly.

"You look hot."

"I know, right?" Cynthia slipped her jacket down a bit on her arms and twirled in the foyer. "I'm going to find me some hottie tonight and ring in the New Year right."

Kylie didn't even bother to hide it when she rolled her eyes. In the last few months since Jax Carver had fallen hopelessly in love with Bria, the beautiful photographer who had shown up at the Springs resort, Cynthia had been on a mission to prove she'd never cared about him anyway. Kylie knew the truth. To Jax, the head chef at the Springs, Cynthia had been nothing more than a diversion, but to Cynthia, it had been a lot more. She tried to hide how much it hurt, but Kylie could see the toll it had taken on her friend.

"And you will definitely find some hotties tonight," Kylie said with an encouraging smile. "Just be good, okay?"

"Speaking of hotties." Cynthia walked through the small apartment and leaned up against Kylie's old couch while she waited for Kylie to pull her stuff together. "Is Marcus going to be there? I heard a rumor that Malcolm had asked him to come back and…"

Kylie stopped listening as her best friend prattled on. She'd frozen at the mention of Marcus's name. She hadn't seen him in almost three years and the last time had been when she thought she'd loved him. He'd been her first love. Or at least, Kylie'd once thought so. But that was a long time ago, before she'd realized what love really was. Before Malcolm.

At least that's what she thought. No. It's what she still thought. Then why were there so many doubts sneaking into her head lately? Why was it that every time Marcus's name was mentioned, her stomach flipped a little? That wasn't supposed to happen.

"Kylie? Hello. Earth to—"

Kylie pushed Cynthia's hand out of her face. "I'm listening. What were you saying?"

"I thought you were listening." Cynthia grinned and wiggled her eyebrows. "Seriously, what's going on with you?"

Kylie turned away, pretending to dig through her purse for a lipstick. Cynthia knew her too well. It would only take one look at her face for her friend to know there was something seriously wrong. And by the sounds of things, she already had a pretty good idea.

"I'm fine." Kylie forced a lightness she didn't feel into her voice. "I'm just so worried about tonight. I should have been up at the hill already to help out with the last-minute details. I told Malcolm I'd talk to the serving staff about the way he wanted things to go tonight and—"

"Seriously? You're supposed to help with the servers? Because you're a waitress? No way."

Kylie spun around, her lipstick in her hand. "It's not like that." But it was like that, wasn't it? That was the whole problem. "He just needed someone who…"

"I was kidding, Kylie." Cynthia's smile was warm and concern creased her face. Damn, but she was sick of people looking at her like that. She was fine. Everything was fine. She was just being ridiculous. "Seriously," Cynthia said, more serious this time. "I was totally kidding. I know that's not how Malcolm operates."

Kylie shook off her concern. "I know. I'm being crazy. I think it's the stress of everything. I'll be fine tomorrow, when all this is behind us and we can get back to normal."

"Exactly." Cynthia grabbed Kylie's jacket and took her hand in a gentle squeeze. "After all, tomorrow is a whole new year. And I can't think of a better time to start fresh."

———

MALCOLM HAD no reason to be worried. Everything was in place for the party. With a little help from his friends, he'd managed to pull off what would be a party people talked about for years. And that's exactly what he wanted. No, what he needed. Running a ski hill wasn't necessarily a lucrative venture, but he was so determined to make Stone Summit a success and if all his market research was on target, he'd be okay. In large part because of the Springs resort a little way down the mountain.

He checked his list for the dozenth time before he glanced at the clock on his desk. He'd brought his tux to the office that morning so he wouldn't need to return to the house because he knew his day would be full of last-minute preparations.

Kylie should have been there by now. She'd insisted on going in to work at the Paw—which was ridiculous on so many levels, Malcolm couldn't keep track. He wished she'd just quit that job. Lord knows she didn't need it, not with everything he had to offer. But it was her thing. She liked it, and whatever made Kylie happy, hell, it made him happy too. It always had.

Even before she was his.

His mind unwillingly went back to the time when Kylie was most definitely not his, but his twin brother's. He didn't want to admit it to anyone, least of all himself, but Marcus had always been a sore spot for him when it came to Kylie, and as much as he missed Marcus and wanted him to be there for the opening, there was part of him, even a very small part, that was definitely nervous about having him back in close quarters with Kylie.

Not that he was worried about Kylie.

Or was he?

He straightened his bow tie in the mirror and wished his beautiful girlfriend was there to do it for him. She should have been there, at his side. That's exactly where he wanted her on his special night.

Too bad she didn't seem to want it, too.

The thought echoed in his head and he tried without much success to shake it off. He'd been too busy working lately, he decided. He'd make it up to her, starting tomorrow, and whatever was bothering her would be okay.

"Tomorrow," he said to his reflection in the mirror. "I'll take care of it tomorrow."

"Talking to yourself, brother? I see nothing's changed."

Malcolm spun around to see his same dark blue eyes staring back at him. "Marcus!" He took the few steps forward to close the space between them and pulled his identical twin into a hug. "It's been too long, brother. Way too long."

"It has." Marcus pulled back and the brothers assessed each other. "But the re-opening of the hill? Hell, you know I'd never miss the chance to shred on this hill again. A lot of fond memories here, brother. A lot." He raised his eyebrow in the cocky gesture that was always all his.

Malcolm knew he was referring to Kylie, but he refused to take the bait. His brother hadn't seemed to care when he'd called and let him know that he was with her now, and after all the years that had passed, why should he? But still, there was still a healthy sense of sibling rivalry between them and Malcolm wouldn't be surprised if Marcus made a play for Kylie, just because he could.

"I'm glad you're here, Marcus." It was the truth. Despite everything, it had been too long since they'd been together. "What do you think of the renos?"

"Well, I'll tell ya, Malc," he slipped easily into his old nickname, "I've been to a lot of hills, all around the world during the boarding circuit and this one...well, it doesn't measure up." He turned and Malcolm saw the shit-eating grin on his brother's face, which prompted him to give him a playful punch in the shoulder. "Seriously, Malc. It's awesome. You did good. So when's the party start?"

"You're not going like that."

Marcus looked down at his jeans and hoodie. "What's wrong with this?"

"It's black tie, Marc."

Marcus pulled a wrinkled tie from his pocket with a flourish. "You're kidding, right?" But Malcolm knew enough to know he wasn't. He shook his head. "It's a good thing I know your size. I ordered you a tux, too."

The brothers were similar in size, but Marcus as a professional snowboarder was leaner, where Malcolm spent most of his time working out in the gym, instead of the hill, and was definitely the bulkier of the two. Despite that, the tux he'd ordered for his brother would fit.

"It's over at the house. I'll get someone to take you over so you can drop off your things." He hadn't been sure of Marcus staying with him because of Kylie, but where else would he stay? Although he hadn't mentioned it to Kylie yet. Surely she must expect it, though.

"I'll stay in one of the rooms for now, Malc. I don't need to—"

"Hell no. You'll stay with me. You're my brother." Besides, he only had a small boutique hotel on the hill, and it was booked for the opening, not that he needed to mention that. "Now grab your stuff. I'll get Sandra to give you a key and I'll see you in a bit."

IT WAS true that most men looked hot in a tux, but when Kylie stepped into Malcolm's office and saw her boyfriend's muscular back standing in the window, looking out over his hill as the sun set, the sight literally took her breath away. When he turned around, and Kylie got the full effect, she could have sworn she swooned a little bit. Sure, she knew how hot her boyfriend was, but Malcolm Stone in a tux—now that was deadly.

"God, you look good." She made her way across the room to him.

He held a hand up and she froze. "Turn," he commanded.

Kylie's knees wobbled a little, and desire flared through her at his authoritative tone, but she did as requested. When she came full circle and her eyes met his again, she could see the desire flaring in his gaze. "Damn, woman. You look positively sinful."

"You like?" She grinned, knowing full well what the answer would be.

He crooked a finger and beckoned her into his arms where she was met with a lip-crushing kiss. "Hell ya, I like," he said when he let her up for air.

It was in moments like this one, held tightly in Malcolm's arms, his desire and love for her radiating through every pore, that Kylie felt like everything between them would be okay. How could she doubt what they had when he so clearly loved her and wanted her, and she wanted him just as badly?

She shouldn't.

"I knew when I saw it, this dress would be sexy as hell on you."

And there it was. The...resentment. She'd been trying to fight it, Lord knows she'd been trying to fight it, but it was just getting worse over time. How was it that the man could make her feel sexy, precious, and desired in one moment and a charity case who needed to be cared for in the next?

She slipped out of his arms, and forced her face to remain neutral. She was getting really good at hiding her feelings, keeping them off her face where he couldn't see that something was wrong. She'd talk to him about it; she would. But not tonight. It could wait. Kylie gave him the sweetest smile she could and reached out to straighten his tie.

Malcolm's gaze softened while she fiddled with his bow tie. The fierce desire from a moment ago was replaced by love and when she finished, he took her hands in his and brought them to his lips. "Thank you."

"Of course. Are you ready for tonight? We should probably go over to the main building. I haven't been there yet and—"

"You haven't spoken to the servers yet?" He dropped her hands and walked to his desk, where he picked up his phone. The ever present phone. Kylie tried not to sigh. "I needed you to look after that for me."

"And I will." She felt her body tense. "I said I would and I will. I just haven't had time. I had to work."

He chuckled. "No you didn't."

Oh no, he was not going to do this. Not now. "I did. It's my job, Malcolm, and I had a shift to work."

He lifted his head; his eyes bored into hers. "I told you, you don't have to work at that pub anymore. In fact, I'd rather you didn't."

He didn't just say that.

"You didn't just say that."

Malcolm shrugged, which only pissed her off more. She knew she should let it go, that she should save her anger for a different day. One that wasn't so important to him. "You would rather I didn't?" Kylie repeated slowly. She couldn't let it go. It had been a sore spot between them for months. One that was just festering and becoming a little more sensitive every day. "What exactly do you mean by that?"

He sighed ever so slightly and tucked his phone into his suit pocket. Of course, it was too much for her to expect that he leave it in his office. Even for one night. Malcolm caught the look she gave his phone. "Don't roll your eyes. I'll need to be reached tonight. It's a big night." He was calm, his voice level, almost annoyingly so as he walked toward her and put his large hands on her waist.

It was a move that usually comforted her, one that had the ability to melt her a little inside. At the moment, it just irritated her.

"Kylie, it is a big night." He tilted her chin so she was looking at him again. "What's going on with you? Is all this getting to you?"

She knew he meant the party and the chaos of the opening, but what he didn't know was that it was more than that. So
much more, she just had no idea how to tell him.

Kylie looked into his eyes. They were so full of love and
concern for her, that once again all her concerns for their relationship bubbled up into feelings of guilt. Any girl would be
ecstatic to be with Malcolm. He was kind, successful, consid-
erate of her feelings, sexy as hell, and he loved her more than
anything.

His cell phone rang.

Well, almost anything.

She dropped her eyes to her shoes.

"Kylie." His voice was full of apology and regret. "I have
to…" He reached into his coat pocket for his phone and she
bit her bottom lip. "It's a big night and I…I have to take this."
He pressed the button to accept the call and Kylie pulled
away.

It was temporary, she told herself for at least the dozenth
time. It wouldn't always be this way. Or would it?

Kylie walked to the window and looked out into the dark
night. It wasn't totally dark; the ski lifts on the front side of the
hill were lit up, and the headlights of the plows grooming the
slopes traveled up and down. It was kind of pretty really, but
Kylie wasn't in the mood to appreciate it.

She listened to Malcolm give orders to whomever he was
talking to on the other end of the phone and she zoned out the
way she always did when he took a call.

What if it didn't get better? Wasn't that the question that was
really bothering her? The one question she couldn't answer.
She glanced over her shoulder at Malcolm, who had his back
to her, his posture stiff with the stress of whatever he was
discussing. *What if he was always a workaholic and put business before
her?* Just like her father.

The thought that she'd been trying to keep from invading

her mind slammed into her with a force that was almost physical.

Growing up, she'd watched her mother slowly shrink into herself more and more every day while her father turned away from her, rejecting her in favor of his work. At first it had just been subtle, little things like working late, or taking a call during dinner. Or maybe those things had just seemed small because she was young. The older she got, the lonelier her mother got. She'd spend more and more time in her bedroom, reading or knitting or doing whatever it was that she did when she was in there. Kylie never was really sure. It was a vicious cycle because the more her mom withdrew, the more her dad stayed away and as an only child, Kylie was in effect—alone.

She'd promised herself she'd never turn out that way. She'd never be the workaholic, married to business the way her father was, and she'd never be her mother, alone among family. So far, she'd managed to avoid turning into her dad. That was easy; she simply never went after a career. It had been easier to wait tables, pick up odd jobs here and there and scrape by, day-to-day. Sure, she'd managed to save a little bit; she wasn't totally broke. But it was nothing like what she could have had.

Success would come at a cost; it always did. Even if she did know what she wanted to do with her life, or more specifically, know how to go about it, she couldn't be sure she'd have enough courage. But it didn't seem to matter because more and more every day, she was turning into her mother.

And she hated every second of it.

But was it like her mother to resent Malcolm for his success? Did her mother resent her father? Or was she happy all those years? Kylie knew if she bothered to ask, Leona Wilson would say no. She'd tell Kylie how hard her father had worked to provide for them and how every day of her marriage, she was thankful for a hardworking man to support her and her child. But Kylie knew she hadn't been happy. It wasn't until her father retired that she'd seen the light come on in her mother again.

"Kylie?"

Malcolm's arms slid around her shoulders and pulled her close against his hard chest. He felt so good, so right, and by reflex, she melted into his embrace.

"Are you okay, babe? You seem a million miles away."

Her head spun with the conflict inside her. Malcolm represented everything she wanted. He loved her and cared for her, and with him, she felt complete. But he also represented so much of what she'd been fighting her whole adult life. The confusion overwhelmed her and she bit back tears.

"Babe?" He trailed his fingers through her hair, and down her neck. His touch was so gentle and soothing; she closed her eyes, and tried to let the feel of him fix the ever expanding hole inside her. "I'm sorry. I know you've put up with so much from me lately," Malcolm continued. "It's been crazy, trying to get everything going, and I know I haven't been fair to you, working so much."

"It's fine."

"No. It's not." He spun her around so she faced him, and tilted her chin up gently so their eyes met. She could see the love for her there and she knew he'd do anything for her. "And I promise I'll make it up to you. After all this craziness is over, let's take some time and get away, just us."

She swallowed down her uncertainty. There was no doubt in her mind that she loved Malcolm and some time alone together would be exactly what they needed. Kylie nodded. "I would like that. A lot."

He kissed her gently on the nose. "Good. Then it's settled. We'll plan something. Soon."

"One more thing," she added before he could move away. He raised an eyebrow in question and she continued, "I know it's going to be busy tonight."

He chuckled. "That's an understatement."

"Promise me that we'll ring in the New Year together."

"Of course we will." He laughed, but Kylie didn't.

"I mean it, Malcolm. It's important to me, okay?"

His laugh died on his lips at her serious tone. "Okay. Of course we will. I promise."

Chapter Three

AS SOON AS they set foot into the main ski lodge that was completely decked out for the party, Malcolm didn't have any time to think about what or what may not be wrong with Kylie. He'd meant what he'd said about trying to find them some time to go away together. Maybe he'd even be able to take her to Eden again? Now, that had been a holiday. The image of Kylie in a tiny bikini popped into his head, laid out on the sand beneath him, heat on her skin and in her eyes.

Yes, he'd like to go back to Eden.

But he'd have to think about it later. Much later. No sooner was he in the building than he was inundated with a flood of people who needed final approval on one thing or another. He'd walked in with Kylie next to him, but when he had a moment to look up, she was gone. Hopefully talking to the serving staff for him. Malcolm prided himself on getting the best of the best for everything. After all, if you were going to do something, might as well do it right the first time. He'd hired the best servers he could find, which happened to be a handful of college kids home for the holidays. They might not be the best of the best, but they were the best around and once

Kylie was done imparting her expert advice to them, Malcolm was confident they'd be fine.

Soon, the light faded from the sky outside, the twinkling lights that the party planners had strung up on what appeared to be every available surface came on, and people began to arrive. Malcolm was caught up in a whirl of people wishing him well, congratulating him and patting him on the back. He'd worked so hard to make the opening of Stone Summit a reality, and finally, it was happening.

"Hey, buddy." Archer Wolfe looked somewhat cleaned up, or as cleaned up as Archer, a self-described mountain man, ever got. He came through the doors and pulled Malcolm into a man hug with a solid slap on the back. "This is some fancy lodge you've got up here. Pretty posh for a ski hill, don't you think?"

Malcolm laughed. Years ago, when they were younger, Malcolm and Archer, along with Marcus, spent all their free time at the old hill, eating their packed bologna sandwiches in the rusty old double-wide trailer that served as the lodge in those days. They'd all come a long way from those days and Archer was right, everything he'd created at Stone Summit was posh in comparison. But he'd make no apologies for it.

"Pretty nice, right?"

"You know it is," Archer said with a grin. "I don't miss that trailer and the watery hot chocolate they used to serve us, one bit."

"Ah, come on, maybe I'll get the cafeteria to water down the cocoa just for you."

"I don't know about cocoa, but I'd settle for a beer."

Together they laughed. One of the best parts of coming back to Cedar Springs—besides Kylie, of course—was reconnecting with Archer. Malcolm had missed the man who was often more of a brother to him than his own twin. It was a good feeling to reconnect.

Together they made their way across the room to the bar and Malcolm got them each a cold beer. They toasted to the success of the hill and each took a long pull.

"You flying solo tonight?" Malcolm asked, although he was pretty sure he knew the answer.

Archer nodded to confirm it.

"On New Year's? You couldn't get a date?"

Archer raised an eyebrow and Malcolm laughed. Of course he could get a date. Archer Wolfe was probably one of the most eligible bachelors in town; women were always throwing themselves at him. The problem was, he didn't seem to want to date anyone. There used to be rumors that Archer might be gay, rumors that had no merit, which Malcolm knew from personal experience. They'd been friends long enough to see Archer with women over the years, but something held him back from finding the right one. Or maybe he'd found her and she wasn't available?

"You know we just want you happy, buddy." Malcolm raised his beer before he tipped it back. "Kylie's always going on about finding you someone so you can settle down and—"

"Where is that woman of yours? Don't tell me she's not here yet? I sent her home hours ago."

"She's here." Malcolm tried to look through the crowd and spot her, but there were too many people, and he couldn't find her. "Somewhere. It's crazy in here."

"It is."

There was something in his friend's voice. Archer wasn't a man of many words, but the words he did use, were meaningful. "What?"

Archer shrugged.

"Is there something you need to say?"

"Not so much something I need to say, but something you need to listen to."

Malcolm gave his friend a sidelong glance. "What the hell does that even mean?"

Archer tipped his beer back and drained it before he put it on the bar behind him. "Just pay attention, man. You have a good woman there."

"I know it." Malcolm made eye contact across the room with Seth, who was trying to get his attention. He moved to step away but Archer's last words caught him.

"Just don't forget it."

———

THE PARTY WAS FUN, and on some level, that kind of surprised Kylie. It shouldn't have; she normally loved parties and hanging out with her friends. It wasn't often that she was partaking in the festivities instead of serving them, but whenever she had the chance, she enjoyed herself. Which was why it shouldn't have been a surprise that she was having a great time at the New Year's festivities. Deep down, of course, she knew she hadn't been looking forward to the night because of everything she was or wasn't feeling about Malcolm, but it had only taken a glass of champagne—or was it two?—and her friends, who were in the party spirit, to turn her around.

Shortly after arriving and Malcolm being swept up by the masses who wanted to talk to him, Kylie slipped away and got herself a drink before she spotted Cynthia at a table in the middle of the room. Leave it to her life-of-the-party best friend to grab the high visibility spot. Kylie joined her at the table and slid into the empty seat next to her. Officer Rhys Anderson and his girlfriend Kari Fox sat across from them, and she gave them a quick wave and smile. She'd noticed before she'd sat down that their other friends, Trent Harrison and his new wife Samantha, were out on the dance floor, lost in each other. She'd missed their wedding a week ago on

Christmas Day because Malcolm couldn't get away from the ski hill.

She still should have gone. Sam was the owner of the Grizzly Paw and had been her boss for years, but more than that, she'd been a good friend. Kylie should have made the trip. With or without Malcolm.

"You can't sit here."

"Thanks." Kylie rolled her eyes, but her friend's words stung a bit. Damn, what was wrong with her lately? It wasn't like her to be so sensitive.

"You know that's not what I meant." Cynthia gave her a gentle smack with the cloth napkin. "You can't sit here because you need to be with that ridiculously good-looking boyfriend of yours, schmoozing and rubbing elbows with…" She took a look around. "Well, with whoever is here who's more important than us." She laughed at her own joke and took another large gulp of champagne.

Maybe that was the key? More champagne. Kylie followed suit and took another sip of her own drink. The bubbles tickled her nose and the alcohol warmed her. She didn't drink very often, which most people found strange considering she worked in a bar, but that was probably the reason. She'd seen more than enough evidence of too much alcohol.

"I'm sure he can handle himself for a few minutes." Kylie took another drink. "Besides, you guys are more fun."

"We are a lot of fun." Rhys raised his glass and the girls laughed.

Kari put a loving hand on his arm and lowered it. "I swear," she said, "I can dress him up…"

"Hey. I don't get to relax and enjoy myself very often. I'm going to enjoy it."

It was true. Because Cedar Springs was such a small town, they didn't have a very large budget for law enforcement, and Rhys spent most of his time working. He swore it was work he enjoyed, and everyone believed him. But still, it was nice to see him kick back and relax a little. Lord knows he deserved it. Kylie snuck a glance at Kari, who had her arm tucked through his and gazed at him the way she always did, with pure love and adoration. She obviously wasn't bothered that her boyfriend was a workaholic, but maybe it was different if it wasn't really by choice, but by need? Was it different? Maybe Kylie should find some time to talk to Kari about how she handled Rhys's long hours.

"And speaking of enjoying it." Rhys put his drink down and jumped to his feet, pulling Kari with him. "I think we should dance."

After the two of them joined the masses on the dance floor, Cynthia spun around and faced Kylie. "Seriously, what is going on with you?"

"What are you talking about?"

"Why aren't you with Malcolm, enjoying every second of being Mrs. Stone Summit? This is his night."

Cynthia's choice of words irked her, but she swallowed down her irritation. "That's just it, Cyn. It's his night. Not mine and I'm not Mrs. Stone Summit."

"You know what I meant."

That was the problem. She did know what Cynthia meant.

"Don't let it bug you, Kylie. It's okay to be part of a couple." Cynthia's pretty face fell and Kylie followed her gaze across the room to where Jax Carver danced with his girlfriend Bria Sheridan. For far too long, Cynthia had held out hope that her and Jax would become...well, something. Now that he was very happily coupled up with Bria, who Kylie had to admit —but not to her friend—was actually his perfect match, Cynthia had been brooding. He wasn't right for Cynthia, never had been. But Kylie was not about to get into that with her friend. Not now anyway.

"You know there are lots of other guys, right? Jax isn't the only one."

"I know." Cynthia shook her pretty head and brought her focus back to Kylie. "And besides that, I'm over him."

Kylie raised a brow.

"I am. And nice try but it's not going to work."

"What are you talking about?" Kylie knew exactly what she was talking about, and it was easier to pretend otherwise. She waved down a server, who looked a little wobbly on her feet, and took another glass of champagne off the girl's tray. Kylie watched her walk away, half expecting the girl to stumble and drop her tray. If Kylie didn't know better, she would think the girl had sampled some of the champagne she'd been serving. With a shrug, she turned back to Cynthia. "I think the server is drunk."

"Stop trying to change the subject."

"I'm not. Seriously, she looks hammered."

"Kylie." Cynthia grabbed her hand and tugged so she looked at her. "Stop worrying about it. Go be with Malcolm. That's what you should be worried about. This is his night, so by default, it's your night. Go and enjoy it." She released Kylie's hand and got to her feet, smoothing her little dress. "I, for one, am going to go find myself a man to ring in the New Year."

She watched Kylie walk away, a swing in her friend's hips, and she had to laugh. There was no doubt, Cynthia would find herself a man. The question was, who?

* * *

MALCOLM HAD JUST FINISHED ACCEPTING the well wishes from Suzy Crosswell—she'd been a fixture in Cedar Springs as long as he could remember—and he was pretty sure he'd just managed to sweet talk her into providing some of her famous cinnamon buns to the coffee shop up at the hill. Kylie would be so impressed; she loved those cinnamon buns. Thinking of his girlfriend, where was she?

He looked around the busy room full of friends and towns-people. People danced, ate, and generally looked to be having a fantastic time. But he couldn't find Kylie anywhere.

A hand, a brotherly hand, smacked down on his shoulder, and startled him. "Quite the party you've got here, Malc."

He turned to see his brother, looking much more put together than he had earlier in the day, standing in front of him.

"Looking good, Marcus. I see you found everything okay?"

"Barely." Marcus laughed. "Such a tiny place you've got, brother." He winked and slapped Malcolm on the back again. Despite everything and the differences they'd had, it was good to have Marcus back again. They'd always been close, even while Marcus had been dating Kylie, and basically treating her so poorly it made Malcolm crazy. But he'd bided his time and ultimately he'd won the girl. For many brothers, it would be a sore spot and a source of anger and resent-ment, but Marcus had never been the kind of guy to be tied down anyway, so it didn't seem to bother him. And if it did, he'd never said a word. To be fair, Malcolm had never asked. He was probably breaking some sort of brother code by being with Kylie, but he didn't care. Not if it meant he got Kylie.

"I'm glad you approve. You can stay as long as you like, but if you want, there'll be a free room in the main lodge in a day or two. It might give you a bit more privacy."

"You mean, it might give you a bit more privacy." Marcus laughed again. "No worries. I'm not looking to cramp your style with Kylie. How is Kylie anyway?"

He couldn't help it; his girlfriend's name coming out of his brother's mouth made Malcolm flinch. "She's fine." Maybe it wouldn't be Marcus who'd have the problem with the situation, but Malcolm?

"I haven't seen her yet." Marcus leaned against the wall and surveyed the room, like a wolf scouting for prey. "I figured she'd be with you."

So had Malcolm, but he wasn't about to admit that. "I'm sure she's busy chatting with the guests and helping me make sure everything goes smoothly. She promised to oversee the serving staff."

"Really?" Marcus raised an eyebrow and gave him a look. "Because she's a waitress?"

Malcolm took a step back as if he'd been slapped. "No. Because she wanted to help."

"With the serving staff? Is she still working at the Paw?"

Malcolm nodded and when Marcus laughed, the sound set him on edge. "What does it matter?"

"No reason, brother." He shook his head, still grinning. "No reason."

One of the servers came around and Marcus grabbed a beer off the tray, nearly causing the boy to drop it. "Steady, buddy. Steady." He turned to Malcolm. "Did you hire a bunch of college kids?"

Malcolm raised a brow as he watched the kid sway his way back to the kitchen and bump into guests along the way.

What the hell?

"Seriously, bro. That kid is drunk. I thought you said you had Kylie in charge of—"

"Shut up." Malcolm's face must have been suitably stern for Marcus to recognize that he meant business because Marcus didn't say another word, but simply gave him a knowing look, which was almost as annoying. "Don't you have something else to do?"

"Not *something* so much as *someone*. I just need to find the lucky lady first."

Malcolm tried not to roll his eyes as Marcus left him behind and sauntered over to the bar in search of someone, likely anyone who would be willing to be his companion for the evening. The thing was, there would be no shortage of women who'd volunteer for the job. Despite the fact that they were identical, Marcus had always been the brother with the ladies falling all over him. Sure, Malcolm had his fair share of girl-friends, too. But there was something about his twin that caused even the most self-respecting of women to trip all over themselves to get closer to him.

Kylie included. The thought was as unexpected as it was unwelcome. The last thing he wanted was to think of his woman with his brother. Nor did he have time for it.

He shoved off the wall he was still reclining on and stalked toward the kitchen in search of the server who was clearly under the influence of something. He'd see him home or put him in the staff room to sleep it off; either way, he needed him off the floor.

As he made his way through the room, he waved and smiled at his friends, promising them he'd be right back to cele-brate with them properly. He'd spent so much time with the local business people who would really help support the ski hill, he'd barely had the chance to say hi to them. Later. He'd deal with the kid, find Kylie, and go say hi. First things first.

The second he pushed through the swinging door into the kitchen, he knew that would have to be much later. The scene he was greeted with was definitely not as simple as what he'd been expecting. Instead of one intoxicated kid, there were at least four of them, slouched over the counter, drinks in hand as they helped themselves to the food they were supposed to be serving.

"What the hell is going on in here?" Malcolm's voice boomed through the stainless steel space, and all four heads shot up. One girl staggered and caught herself before she crashed into a cart full of plates.

"Mr. Stone. We were…just…" A boy—Caleb, if Malcolm remembered properly—spoke up. He was clearly trying his best to appear sober. An effort that wasn't succeeding.

"You were just helping yourself to my liquor and food?" He took a few steps toward the kids, his anger radiating out of him. He knew he could be an intimidating man, especially when he was angry. He knew he probably should step back, but despite knowing all of that, he took another step forward.

Caleb, full of liquid courage, stood straight and nodded. "It was just a few drinks…it is New Year's, after all, and Kylie said—"

"Quiet."

The boy snapped his mouth shut.

What the hell had Kylie said? And where the hell was she? She was supposed to be looking after the kids. Had she told them they could have a drink or two? Malcolm took a deep breath and tried to steady himself. She probably had. She didn't understand the importance of the evening. Dammit.

"I don't care what Kylie may or may not have told you. It really doesn't matter. This isn't her event. I'm in charge here."

"Malcolm!"

He turned to see Kylie, looking extremely sexy and even more pissed off, standing in the doorway.

Chapter Four

HAD he just said that it didn't matter what she'd said? That it wasn't her event and she wasn't in charge? He'd seriously just told the serving staff, the serving staff that she was in charge of, that it didn't matter what she'd said. Kylie shook with anger and hurt. Looking at Malcolm in that moment, towering over the kids who were definitely drunk and perilously close to ruining his party, she probably should have sympathized with him. But it was the serving staff she related to and instinctively sided with.

"I don't think yelling at them is going to do any good." She managed to get the words out with as much control over her voice as she could summon. "Caleb, take everyone to the staff room and make a pot of coffee." She turned and looked pointedly at Malcolm. "If that's okay with you, that is?"

With his mouth in a firm line, Malcolm nodded tersely. He waited until the kids were gone before he said anything else, but as soon as the door swung shut behind them, he turned and looked at her.

"Now what the hell am I supposed to do?"

"They couldn't serve in that state."

"You were supposed to be looking after them."

She flinched at the words, but she wasn't going to back down. She was not his staff.

"I don't work for you."

"You said you'd—"

"Talk to them," she said through clenched teeth. She might be a full foot shorter than him, but when she got fired up, she wasn't to be messed with, and Kylie had definitely had enough, and maybe just enough champagne to make her bold. "And I did that. But unless I'm mistaken, I'm not on your payroll. Am I?"

He ran a hand through his dark hair, a move he only did when he was stressed or aggravated. "Kylie, you're being ridiculous. Of course you're—"

"No?" She crossed her arms in front of her chest, mostly to keep them from shaking. "Then why do you insist on acting like I am?"

He took a step toward her and in that moment, she wanted nothing more than to connect with him, but at the same time she needed him to keep his distance so she didn't cave. Of course, the second he put his hand on her shoulder, the heat from his touch melted her a little.

"Kylie." He put his other hand on her other shoulder and squeezed gently, pulling her into him. "It's not like that. You know that."

She shook her head and nodded at the same time. She did know that. Or did she just want to know that? She was so confused.

"I know." Her words came out as a whisper, likely because she didn't really believe them.

He put a gentle kiss on the top of her head, and Kylie felt her anger and resolve to tell Malcolm everything she was feeling evaporate. "Good," he said. "Because you know I really need some help now, right?"

Her entire body went rigid at his words and she took one quick step backward to put just enough distance between them. "Of course you do." The words were forced and clipped.

Malcolm searched her face, but if he found anything out of the ordinary in her expression, he didn't say anything.

"Okay," he said slowly. "I knew you'd understand."

He didn't say anything outright and he didn't have to. Kylie could see exactly what was going on in Malcolm's head. She knew where she stood. Hot anger coursed through her, and before she could think it through, Kylie grabbed one of the black serving aprons from the counter and tied it around her waist before she picked up a serving tray. She curtsied deep, just to hammer the point home. "Anything you need, Mr. Stone."

Before he could say another word, she pushed out through the kitchen doors and back to the party to fulfill her role. The only role Malcolm had ever seen her as.

KYLIE HAD NEVER BEEN one to cry in public, and she certainly didn't plan to cry in front of all her friends at the *party of the year*, but she wasn't made of stone. Walking out of the kitchen and away from Malcolm had fractured her, but not nearly as much as the fact that he hadn't come after her.

There was no point dwelling on it.

"Can I grab a drink?"

A woman Kylie didn't recognize appeared next to her and gestured to the glasses of champagne Kylie had just stocked her tray with. She must have been from out of town—Kylie didn't recognize her—and she obviously thought she was just the serving staff. Which, at the moment, given what had just gone down in the kitchen, she was.

"Of course." Kylie forced a smile. "I was just getting ready to bring them around."

The woman nodded and slipped a dollar bill onto Kylie's tray. She had to swallow hard to keep from calling her back and returning her tip. She may have made a scene with Malcolm, but she wouldn't stoop to making a scene in front of the entire party. She tucked the bill in her apron.

"What the hell are you doing?" Cynthia appeared next to her. "You're supposed to be at the party, not working it."

"I think circumstances have changed."

"How so?" Cynthia put an arm out to stop her, but the look on Kylie's face must have changed her mind. "What the hell, Kylie? What's going on? Where's Malcolm?"

She picked up the tray and stopping short of heaving it up on her shoulder bar room style, she held it in front of her and walked away before calling over her shoulder, "No doubt enjoying *his* party."

Of course, she could have just walked out. She didn't need to take on the role, but she loved Malcolm. And even though he was being a first-class asshole and she wasn't even sure anymore whether their relationship would make it through this latest and biggest setback, she couldn't find it in herself to leave him high and dry.

She filled the next little while serving drinks with the remaining sober servers, and avoiding questions and concerned looks from her friends. Soon enough, Slade Black took the stage and everyone seemed to forget about why or why not Kylie may have assumed the role of waitress. Slade was the latest *it* guitar player, who also happened to be engaged to Beth Martin, longtime Cedar Springs resident and one of Kylie's friends, so of course he'd agreed to play at the New Year's party. Everyone loved him, especially his new solo songs that he'd written since leaving his band the Jacked Crackers and meeting Beth.

Kylie snuck off to the corner to refill her tray and listen to the music for a moment. She hadn't let herself slow down long enough to look for Malcolm, purposely keeping herself busy enough so she wouldn't be tempted to search him out and see what he was doing. He didn't come to her. He hadn't tried to talk to her. To apologize to her. Nothing. It was that fact that hurt her the most.

With her refill complete, Kylie looked up from the tray where she'd just stacked another set of full champagne glasses and directly at Malcolm. She'd held out some sort of hope that he might be as hurt as she was. That maybe he was off somewhere thinking about what had gone down between them and how they could fix it. But he wasn't doing any of those things. He was laughing and smiling with their friends. Enjoying his party the way he should be. But without her. The tears she'd fought since their confrontation threatened to spill over and she swiped at them, forcing them to stay back. The action must have caught his eyes, because Malcolm looked in her direction. Instead of his face clouding with the same hurt she was feeling, his eyes dropped quickly—to the full tray, no doubt—and he nodded before he smiled the same charismatic smile she usually loved. This time, the sight filled her with pain but she wouldn't let him see it. Not now. She swallowed the hurt and lifted the tray, purposely headed in the opposite direction.

By the time she'd emptied her tray, the countdown was approaching. She handed two full bottles to the servers she had left and gave them instructions to top up every glass they saw. She couldn't bring herself to make the rounds again. Not so close to the New Year. Instead, Kylie took a full bottle to herself. As she tipped it back and took a hefty drink, the bubbles tickled the back of her throat. Really, what was the point of doing anything else?

She slipped to the side of the bar, close to the kitchen door where she could make a hasty getaway if it was needed, and scanned the room. She couldn't find Malcolm. Did she want to?

They'd promised to ring in the New Year together and tradition said that the first person you kissed would be the one you would be with all year. She should be with him. Only, she wasn't sure she wanted to be. She tipped back the bottle again and let the alcohol warm her belly.

Slade had stopped singing now and stood in the middle of the stage. He had his arm around Beth, holding her close, and Beth's daughter Jules stood on his other side. "I'm going to get someone very special to help me with the countdown this year," he spoke into the microphone. "Jules?"

The teenager girl smiled shyly before she took the microphone in two hands and commanded it as though she'd done it her whole life.

"Ten!"

Still a whole ten seconds left in the year. She'd definitely need more alcohol. Kylie took another drink.

"Nine."

She kept her eyes closed, letting the bubbles pop in her mouth. Champagne really wasn't so bad. She could get used to this.

"Eight."

Kylie opened her eyes, not sure what she was looking for anymore.

"Seven."

Her friends were all paired off with their significant others. Slade and Beth stood on the stage, their arms wrapped around each other, eyes firmly locked on each other.

"Six."

Trent and Samantha in the middle of the dance floor. Rhys and Kari next to them, ready to ring in the New Year with the ones they loved.

"Five."

Another big pull from the bottle.

"Four."

Malcolm. He'd appeared on the other side of the room. Had he been there the whole time?

"Three."

He tilted his head in question and nodded with a grin. She knew him well enough to know that he thought she'd come when he requested.

"Two."

She wanted to cross the floor to him, but there was no way. She couldn't.

"Kylie? What are you—"

"One!"

She didn't think but acted purely on instinct, turning at the familiar voice and the sound of her name, directly into his arms. His arms came up around her in reflex, his lips on hers by…what? Memory? Instinct?

Either way, it wasn't Malcolm Stone who kissed her into the new year: it was Marcus, his twin brother and her ex-boyfriend.

"COME ON." Someone put a hand on Malcolm's shoulder, stopping him mid-step as he started to cross the room. "You don't want to do that."

Malcolm turned, ready to punch whoever dared stop him from pulling his woman away from his brother's grasp.

Archer.

Of course it would be Archer.

"Let me go," Malcolm growled. "You do not want to get in my way right now."

Archer might be big, but he was no match for Malcolm at the moment.

But his friend wasn't letting go. He tugged on Malcolm's shoulder again and yanked him back. "Do you really want to do this in front of everyone right now?" Malcolm stared at him. "Think about it, Malcolm. You don't want to do this."

His shoulders sagged, and Archer took the opportunity to pull him out of the room and into the cold air outside.

"What the hell was that?" Malcolm stalked off into the snow. He had no idea where he was going, but he knew Archer was right; he needed to get away from the party and what he'd just seen. "What the hell was she thinking?"

Blind rage overtook him and he slammed his fist into the wood siding. Ignoring the pain in his hand, he did it again and again, before Archer grabbed him.

"If you have to, hit me."

Malcolm turned slowly and stared openmouthed at his friend. "What?"

"You're not going to feel better unless you hurt someone and I'm certainly not going to let you walk into that party and punch your twin brother in front of everyone. Particularly since it's your party and he's kind of the celebrity guest. Not happening."

"I'm not punching you."

"Do it."

Archer squared up and dropped his hands next to his side. The thought tempted Malcolm for a second, and his fingers curled instinctively back into a fist.

If it hadn't been for the pain that had started to become apparent in his bloodied knuckles, he might have taken him up on the offer. Instead, he dropped his hand and swore.

In silence, Archer handed him a pack of snow and he put it on his hand.

After a moment, Malcolm shook his head. "I don't even know what to say. Why would she do that?"

"You don't think she mistook him for you, do you?"

"Really?"

Archer shrugged. "I don't know, man. It's dark in there; she's probably had a few drinks and…"

"No."

That was the problem. Malcolm was positive Kylie wouldn't mistake them. She'd done that once, years ago, when she'd been dating Marcus. That situation had worked out in Malcolm's favor ultimately, but no. There was no way she'd make that mistake again.

And that's why it hurt so badly.

Kylie would have known exactly who she was kissing.

"Go back in, Archer."

"No way. I'm not letting you beat up on your new ski lodge. Someone has to defend it."

Despite himself, Malcolm chuckled. "I'm not going to punch the building. Or anything or anyone, for that matter."

Archer didn't look as if he believed him at all, and hell, if he were Archer he wouldn't have believed him either, but it was true. All he wanted was to be alone. "I mean it, Arch. I'm not going back in there. Don't worry."

"You need to talk to her."

"No."

"Malcolm, don't be a dick."

"Really?" The anger he'd only barely suppressed flared up again. "I'm being a dick? Really? Me." The anger left almost as soon as it had arrived and he slumped his shoulders. "Just go, Archer. If she has anything to say to me, she can come and find me."

They stood in silence for a few minutes. Each of them looked up to the night sky. The cold air pierced through his suit jacket, and he knew Archer, who wore only a dress shirt, must be frozen, but neither man would back down.

"You're sure?" Archer asked after a few minutes. He knew Malcolm well enough to know when to back away. He also knew when he wasn't going to win. "You're going to be okay?"

Malcolm nodded. "I'm good."

Archer nodded tersely and smacked him on the back. "Happy New Year, buddy."

"Happy New Year."

He didn't turn, but he listened to Archer's footfalls crunch in the snow as he left him alone. "Happy New Year," he whispered into the night as he once again pictured his brother's arms around Kylie, his lips on hers were his own should have been.

"Happy fucking New Year." He kicked a chunk of snow and stalked off. He needed a drink, and the only place to get it was by going back inside. And if Kylie was there, well...they had a lot to talk about.

IT TURNED OUT, by the time he'd returned, Kylie was gone. After a quick scan of the room, it appeared Marcus was missing as well. He didn't want to think about what that meant. Kylie wouldn't do that to him. She would never—but they had been together once and this is the first time since they broke up that they'd seen each other. What if those feelings were still there?

Damn.

That was exactly what he'd been worried about.

He made a beeline to the bar and poured himself a whiskey, which he downed before he poured himself another one.

"Happy New Year, Malcolm." Cynthia appeared by his side and gave him a hug and a kiss on the cheek as soon as he turned.

He mumbled something in response, not caring if it made sense.

"Where's Kylie? I want to wish her a happy New Year, too. I haven't seen her."

"You haven't?" Maybe nobody had seen what went down.

Cynthia shook her head. "No. No one has."

Malcolm picked up his drink and held it aloft. "Well, add me to that list." He toasted the air and swallowed the contents of his glass.

"Everything okay? You look…"

"What?"

Cynthia took a step back. He hadn't meant to snap at her, but he was too far gone to apologize. "Nothing," she said tersely. "Never mind."

To his relief, before she could say anything else, a man he only vaguely recognized as one of the lift operators appeared and slid his arm around her waist to pull Cynthia onto the dance floor. "Tell her I'm looking for her," she called as she went.

"You and me both." He poured another glass full, determined to numb whatever he was feeling.

Chapter Five

KYLIE WOKE up with her head pounding and a queasiness in her stomach that had less to do with the champagne she'd consumed the night before, but more to do with her behavior the night before. Sure, she drank way too much, but she still knew what she was doing.

Maybe it would have made it easier if she had been so drunk that she didn't realize it was Marcus who stood next to her, put his arms around her, his lips to hers…yes, that would have been easier.

But the fact was, she did know. And she'd still done it.

Tentatively, she opened one eye and looked around. She was in her own bed. Alone.

Not that she expected to be anywhere else, or with anyone else. Not really.

After she'd kissed Marcus, she hadn't waited around to see if anyone, namely Malcolm, had seen what she'd done. What was the point? She hadn't kissed Marcus to get a reaction out of his brother. Had she?

She was so not ready to face the day and the fallout she

knew there'd be, so she pulled the comforter over her head and rolled over. Her head spun and her stomach revolted.

Without letting the light in under the covers, Kylie reached out and grabbed her cellphone. Four missed calls.

Malcolm.

Her chest hurt just thinking of him. He must have seen what she'd done.

But he hadn't stopped it.

Who was she kidding? There was no way he hadn't seen it. She'd all but made sure he wouldn't miss it.

God. She was such a bitch.

The problem was, in the hours before she'd finally fallen into a restless sleep, she'd lain awake racking her brain for an explanation or even the lamest of reasons that would explain why she would kiss Marcus. Especially when she knew it was the one thing that would really hurt Malcolm.

And the only reason she could come up with was just that. It would really hurt Malcolm.

But it didn't make any sense. Why would she want to hurt the man she loved?

Kylie punched in the code for her voicemail and braced herself for Malcolm's angry voice. She'd been a chicken and run off as soon as she could the night before; there was no doubt that made him even angrier. Just the way she was being a coward now and avoiding the question to herself. She knew why she would want to hurt him. Even on a subconscious level.

The electronic voice announced message one of four messages.

"Happy New Year!" Cynthia's voice screeched into the phone, the familiar sounds of the party in the background. "Where are you? I want to kiss you and hug you."

Kylie had to laugh. Typical Cynthia, celebrating in style. She hadn't been paying attention, but there was no doubt she'd found herself someone to help her ring in the New Year.

The same voice announced the second message.

"Seriously? Where are you? I want you to meet...wait, what's your name? Brett. I want you to meet Brett. He's a—"

Kylie smiled. Definitely, her best friend had a good night.

Her smile faded as the third message was announced. Certainly, this one would be Malcolm.

"Kylie. Really? Where are you?" Cynthia sounded a lot more sober, and a whole lot more worried. "I can't find you anywhere and Malcolm is...well, call me, okay? I'm getting worried."

She swallowed down the guilt that rose up and listened to the last message, somehow knowing this one wouldn't be Malcolm either.

"What is going on? Are you okay? Did you and Malcolm have a fight? He's totally incoherent and his fist is all bloodied up and...where are you, Kylie? I'm going to start getting really worried. Call me!"

Kylie tossed the phone aside and buried her face in the pillow.

He'd seen the kiss. There was no doubt Malcolm knew what had happened and she couldn't be sure whether she was upset that he hadn't called to confront her, or relieved.

IT TOOK her another hour to work up the physical and mental strength to get out of bed and into the shower, but the moment the hot water hit her, she was glad she'd made the effort. The water cleansed her and slowly her head cleared so she could think straight.

As Kylie lathered her hair, she replayed the night before in her mind. Everything except for the kiss. She didn't want to think about the kiss.

Or she did.

She couldn't decide what was worse, which was exactly why she didn't want to think about it. The first thing she needed to do was talk to Malcolm.

And do what?

Apologize? Certainly.

But then what? What would she say? And really, what was there to say? The longer she spent in the shower, the more convinced she was that even though what she'd done had been wrong on so many different levels, she didn't really feel all that bad about it. At least not as bad as she should have.

And didn't that tell her something?

Yes. It told her a lot and she knew what she had to do when she found Malcolm.

Kylie took her time blow-drying her hair and getting dressed, but finally she couldn't procrastinate any more. She found her car keys in the bottom of her purse. By some miracle, she'd been able to catch a ride down the mountain and back to town with a couple who wasn't staying to celebrate the New Year any longer. Something about their babysitter calling and a sick kid. To be fair, Kylie hadn't asked for details. She just needed to get home and quickly.

She would have liked to stop in at Dream Puffs to grab a latte and a cinnamon bun, but the chance of running into someone who might have seen what she'd done, or at least noticed that she hadn't been there for Malcolm, was too much. She couldn't face it. No, it was easier if she took care of what she needed to. Kylie didn't even have to think about where to go. There was only one place Malcolm would be on the first day of the year: the ski hill. She navigated her car up the snowy roads, taking her time around the corners. A fresh layer of snow had fallen and it didn't look as if the sander had been out yet.

When she got to the ski hill, she pulled over to the side of the road. If she took the main road, it would lead to the

parking lots and buildings. The side road would take Kylie to
Malcolm's chateau. If he'd really been drinking too much,
there was a chance he'd be sleeping off a hangover. She looked
down the snowy road, lined with pine trees. The houses were
around the bend, each of them secluded just enough from the
next one. They all backed onto the hill, so you could ski in and
out. The views were breathtaking and Malcolm's house was the
loveliest of them all.

Malcolm's house.

Despite him insisting that she move in, she never had. It
never felt right. And now…she shook her head as she put the
car in drive and turned the car the other way, toward the main
lodge and offices. Malcolm would be working. There'd never
really been any doubt.

She passed all the cars in the parking lot and smiled at the
sight of the hill covered in people. It was a beautiful day for
skiing. Not too cold and with a light dusting of snow falling.
Malcolm would be pleased and she was pleased for him. The
hill would be a success. She knew it. But along with the smile,
there was a heaviness in her heart as she pulled up next to
Malcolm's car.

It was pointless, but she checked her phone anyway just to
see whether Malcolm had called while she was driving. Still
nothing.

With a sigh, Kylie grabbed up her purse and headed into
the office. She hadn't expected to see Sandra working; after all,
it was a holiday and sure enough, the front office was empty.
She made her way to the ajar door and pushed it slightly so it
swung open. He had his back to her and it took a moment to
see whether he was sleeping or working. She waited, biding her
time and enjoying watching him in silence.

"Kylie."

The sound of his voice took her off guard. She expected
him to be angry. Instead, he sounded tired. Defeated.

"Come in."

He still didn't turn around and after a pause, she stepped forward. "Malcolm? Can we talk?"

Finally, he turned around and the moment she saw his face, she knew that whatever she thought she was going to say wasn't going to be enough.

"I think we should," he said. "Talk, I mean. I'm just not sure there's anything to say."

He nodded to the chair across from him, but she opted to stand. Something about him sitting in his chair behind his desk seemed to give him an advantage. An advantage to what, she couldn't be sure. After all, weren't they on the same side? Didn't they want the same things?

"Of course there's something to say. Malcolm, I—"

"You what?" His face was hard, his eyes dark. "You're sorry? You didn't mean it? It didn't mean anything that you were kissing my twin brother on New Year's? Is that what you're trying to say?"

She swallowed hard, taken back by his vehemence. "Yes, I'm—you know what?" Anger boiled up in her. Yes, she screwed up. She made a mistake and she did something she shouldn't have, but she'd be damned if she was going to stand here and let him put all of their problems on her.

"What? You're not sorry?"

She shook her head and squeezed her arms tightly around her middle. "No. I mean, yes. I'm sorry for what I did. I didn't even realize I was doing it, and…it doesn't matter. I'm not going to make any excuses for my behavior. It shouldn't have happened. But this is not all my fault."

"Really?" He leaned back in his chair and crossed his arms over his chest. Logically, she knew he was being defensive and trying to protect himself from being hurt, but logic had no place in a fight.

"Yes, really." She stood strong, suddenly determined to let him know exactly how she felt.

"And how exactly is it my fault at all?" He laughed, but it was not a happy sound. "Please tell me, how exactly is it my fault that you kissed Marcus? This should be good. I mean, you have been waiting to kiss him ever since he walked out on you, haven't you? All this time, Kylie—it's always been him, hasn't it?"

"What?" She shook her head. "No."

"It's never been about me and you, has it? It's always been Marcus you wanted. When we're together, and—"

"Malcolm! Stop it."

"It's true, isn't it?"

"No." She shook her head again and took a step forward. "Is that what you think? Really?"

When he didn't answer right away, she knew it to be true. "You can't really think that I'm with you because of Marcus. After everything we've been through and..." She faded away, because they hadn't really been through much. At the first sign of trouble and unhappiness, what had she done? She certainly hadn't turned to him and tried to talk it out like she should have. No, she'd pretty much done the worst thing she could have done. Unable to look at him any longer, Kylie turned away. "I'm only going to say this one more time." Her voice was low, but she knew he could hear her. "I'm not with you because of Marcus. I was with you in spite of him."

"What do you mean *was*?"

"What?" She turned around again. This time the look on his face almost broke her. The anger was gone; he once again looked sad, and so broken. Her gut twisted with the knowledge that she'd done that to him.

He pushed up from his chair and came around the desk. "You said *was*," he repeated. "You said you were with me in spite of him. What did you mean by *was*?"

She shook her head by reflex. "I didn't mean—" Or did she?

"This is just a fight, Kylie." He stepped toward her and took her hand. "Isn't it?"

She couldn't look at him. Every uncertainty and question she'd had for the last few months surfaced. Was it just a fight? Something they could work their way through? Or was it more? Had she kissed Marcus as a way to get out of the relationship? A relationship where she never quite felt good enough?

"Kylie?" He squeezed her hand. "What's going on?"

"I shouldn't have kissed him," she said, her voice slightly more than a whisper. "And I know you don't believe me, but I didn't mean to. I didn't plan it. I saw you there, and I was wait-ressing and I didn't want to be because it was your party and I should have been at your side, not serving all our friends but you only ever see me as a waitress because that's all I've ever been and it's all I'll ever be and you're successful and a business owner and you deserve to be with someone better than me and I…" Tears slid from her eyes and splashed over their hands. She looked up then and through a veil of tears, said what she'd wanted to say for months. "I deserve to be with someone who sees me for more than what I am and can see all that I could be."

"Kylie, I do. You know I do."

"No." She shook her head violently and sniffed loudly. She knew she was being messy, but sometimes feelings were messy and now that she'd started to talk, she couldn't stop. "You don't. You want me to quit my job and take care of me because what I do isn't as important as what you do, and maybe it's not. But it's mine. And maybe I don't want to be a waitress for the rest of my life, but you wouldn't know that because you've never asked. You've just assumed that I'll go along with whatever you want to do, but I won't, because I will not be a kept woman, Malcolm. I need my own things, my own identity. I...I won't turn into my mother, Malcolm. I can't." She yanked her hands from his and wiped at her face.

"What are you talking about? This isn't about what you do for a living. If you want to do something else, then I'll make sure—"

"No." She held up a hand. "That's the problem. You want to do it for me. You want to take care of me because you don't think I can do it on my own."

"That's not it at all. Christ, Kylie." Malcolm ran his hands through his hair and paced over to the window. "I thought we were fighting about last night. Look, I know you were drinking and—"

"Don't make excuses for me."

"I'm not."

"You are."

He shook his head and clenched his fists before he released them. Kylie could see the frustration building and she knew she was being unreasonable, but she couldn't seem to stop herself.

"Then you tell me," he said after a moment. "Where do we go from here?"

She could have said a million things. She could have told him they needed to talk it through, that they needed to spend some time discussing the future and making plans. She could have taken him in her arms and kissed him until they both forgot what they were fighting about, and made love on his desk. She could have done any one of those things. But instead, she said, "I think we should take a break."

WHAT THE HELL had she just said? A break? What the fuck did that mean?

"A break?"

55

She nodded and took another step away from him.

"You mean from…"

"Each other, yes."

"No." He crossed his arms and shook his head. "That's not an option." Whatever she was thinking, there was no way he was going to let her make this terrible mistake. Not after everything they'd been through in finding each other again after all those years. Hell no. Not happening.

"Malcolm." Her voice was quiet, but strong. The shaking and uncertainty was gone, as if her grand announcement had given her strength, but that was ludicrous. This whole conversation was ludicrous. They'd been fighting over her kissing Marcus. How the hell had they gone from that to a break?

Unless? No. He refused to think it had anything to do with his brother being back in town. The question must have shown on his face, because Kylie said, "This is about us. It has nothing to do with Marcus."

"Then why? It doesn't make any sense." He took a step toward her at the same time she retreated. "Kylie, this is ridiculous. We're having an argument. It's not a reason to break up."

"Not a breakup. A break."

"Same thing."

"No." She shook her head, but wouldn't meet his eyes. "It's not. I just need some time to figure things out. I need some space."

With one big step, he crossed the distance, grabbed her by the shoulders, and forced her to look at him. "What if I can't give you space?" The idea of her pulling away from him caused him physical pain. He couldn't lose her. He wouldn't lose her. "I won't let you…" He trailed off. He wasn't going to frighten her into staying. That wasn't his style and he'd never hurt her. Never.

"Malcolm." Her eyes glistened with tears again. "You have

to. Please." The word was a plea and he released her. She took a stumbling step backward.

"I love you, Kylie." He struggled to keep his voice even. "I can't lose you. Not like this."

"You're not losing me." Tears streamed down her face. He stuffed his hands in his pocket to keep from reaching out and taking her pain away. "This isn't permanent, it's just…"

"A break." He repeated the empty words, and it brought a small smile to her face. A broken, sad smile, but a smile nonetheless.

"Thank you for understanding."

She turned and left his office before he could say that he didn't understand. He didn't understand at all. He waited until he heard the door to the front office shut and only then did he allow himself to pick up the ceramic pencil holder on his desk and hurl it at the wall where it shattered, scattering the pens and pencils inside.

She'd said he wasn't losing her, but if that was true, why did it hurt so fucking bad?

WITH NOTHING TO do and nowhere to go, Malcolm grabbed his ski equipment from the closet and headed out to the hills in an effort to clear his head. Sitting in his office would only make him crazy and he couldn't go down to town. The last thing he wanted was to talk to anyone. He currently couldn't go home. Marcus might be there. He hadn't shown up the night before; he was obviously smarter than that and no doubt he'd found some poor young woman to hook up with. Unless…no. He wouldn't allow himself to think that Kylie and Marcus had… no. And sure, she'd insisted that the break or whatever the hell it was had nothing to do with him, but he didn't believe her. Not really.

The snow was fresh and fluffy in the trees were the groomers didn't go and that's where Malcolm headed. With any luck, he could find some untracked powder after the snow-fall from the night before. He waved at the liftie, but didn't encourage conversation and to his relief got a chair to himself. Perks of being the boss. The moment his skis landed on the snow at the top of the mountain, he pushed off and headed for the back of the mountain and the runs that were usually fairly empty and reserved for advanced skiers.

He pushed his body hard, skiing as fast as he could, cutting tight around the trees. He knew the lines he always took and even if he did run into an obstacle, he didn't care. When he came up on the rocky cliff that he knew opened out onto a soft clearing, he pushed even harder and jumped into the air, twisting his skis, and enjoyed the cold air whip his face. He landed the jump hard and continued down the run.

Malcolm was a good skier. Where his brother had chosen snowboarding, and had eventually gone pro, Malcolm preferred two skis beneath his feet. He'd been good enough once to go pro, too. But he'd always wanted more than that for his future. Being a ski bum would have been a fun life, living the thing he loved more than anything, but what kind of finan-cial security would there have been in it? No. Malcolm wanted more than a life of traveling from hill to hill, making extreme skiing videos. He'd wanted a home and a good woman to share it with. Kylie. He'd always wanted Kylie.

A lot of good that had done him. Now here he was, skiing through the trees, alone.

He would have laughed at the irony, but instead he pushed harder. Turned tighter. Forced his skis to go faster. When he finally broke out of the trees, he turned hard, coming to a stop in a spray of snow. He dropped his hands to his knees and sucked hard for a breath.

"Nice rip."

Malcolm looked up to see Seth on a snowmobile a few feet away.

"I haven't seen someone ski like that since...well, since I saw you ski years ago. You haven't lost your touch, man, and if I didn't know better I'd think you were trying to out-ski some demons or something. What got into you? That was insane."

Malcolm shook his head. His heart slowly returned to a normal beat. "Nothing. Just out for a ski, man."

"You sure that's it?"

Malcolm and Seth had always been friendly, but they'd never been super close. He had Marcus and Archer for that. A lot of good having Marcus had been. Just thinking of his brother made him fume, but it wasn't his fault. Logically, he knew that.

Fuck logic.

"Seriously," Seth said. "Are you okay?"

Malcolm forced his breathing back to normal and worked hard to make sure his face was as neutral as possible. He assessed the man in front of him. Sure, he'd find out sooner or later what had happened with Kylie. But as far as he was concerned, it could be later. "It's all good, Seth. Sorry. I just have a lot on my mind. What are the numbers today? They should be up, am I right?"

Seth gave him a strange look and for a moment, Malcolm was worried he was going to push the issue. He didn't. Instead, he nodded and filled Malcolm in on the conditions and early sales figures for the day. It was easy for Malcolm to shift into business mode, to push his personal issues aside, and compartmentalize them in a box he'd worry about later. He focused on what Seth was telling him and soon his head was full of data and numbers that surprised him in a good way.

But even as their conversation wrapped up and Seth took off on his machine, headed for the mid-way ski patrol lodge, Malcolm couldn't completely clear his head of everything.

Usually losing himself in his work allowed him the chance to clear his head from everything else, but it wasn't working. In fact, he realized he hadn't really retained anything Seth had told him. The entire time Seth had been talking, the only thing Malcolm could focus on was Kylie and how just yesterday she'd been standing next to him on the hill, smiling and laughing and looking sexy as hell in her ski jacket before she matched him turn for turn down the slope and now, he was alone. And he had no idea how it had all gone so wrong, so quickly.

Chapter Six

FOR JANUARY, it was a beautiful day, with only the slightest hint of snow hanging in the air. Normally Kylie would love walking to work on such a day, taking her time, enjoying the blue sky and the fresh air. But she couldn't enjoy the day. She couldn't enjoy anything. It had been only three days since Kylie had told Malcolm she wanted a break. She hadn't meant to say the words; she hadn't even been thinking about a break. In fact, had anyone asked her what she wanted, that would have been the last thing she ever would have suggested. That's why she couldn't understand why the words had slipped so easily from her mouth or more telling, why the minute she'd spoken them, she'd felt an immediate sense of relief settle over her.

Even after she'd explained everything to Cynthia, she'd been confused. Maybe more so. She felt good. Mostly. She also felt empty.

Was it possible to feel relief and disappointment at the same time?

She'd spent most of the days since *the break* with Malcolm expecting him to call or drop in while she was at work. But he hadn't. In fact, she hadn't even caught a glimpse of him or his

SUV around town. Nobody mentioned him at the Grizzly Paw, at least not in front of her. It was strange. As if he'd gone out of town, or totally disappeared. But she missed him.

She kicked at a chunk of snow on the sidewalk. "Don't be stupid, Kylie," she reprimanded herself and glanced around. No doubt if anyone saw her or overheard her, word would get around that she'd totally lost her mind, but she didn't care. It's not as if they weren't already talking about her. "This was all your idea. You have to live with it."

"What was your idea?"

The voice startled her, but not as much as the person attached to the voice. Of course, she'd known she would run into him. It was a small town, but seeing him, she had to do a double take. Damn, he looked so much like his brother that it made her heart skip a beat. "Marcus."

"I can't tell if you're happy or disappointed to see me."

She forced her face to look as neutral as possible, especially considering she didn't know either. He was dressed in a bright blue snowboarding parka that fell past his waist, and his eyes were hidden behind dark sunglasses.

"I guess I assumed you left town," she finally managed to say.

"Why do you think I would do that?" Marcus slid his glasses off his face and looked her squarely in the eye. The second he did that, she wished he would put them back on. She didn't want to look in his eyes and see the glint there that had never failed to make her stomach flip. For identical twins, they were still so different, and that confident way of looking at her as if she was his to have his way with, that was Marcus's alone. When they'd been together, no matter what his crimes against their relationship had been, she'd forgive him the second he looked at her like that and he knew it.

Kylie shook her head and looked away. It had been a long

time since he'd looked at her like that, and just as long since she'd responded to it. A lot had changed. It wouldn't work.

"Just with...with everything...I assumed..." She hated herself for the uncertainty in her voice. She cleared her throat, turned to face him and tried again. "I guess I thought you might not have a place to stay."

"You mean because of Malcolm and the whole..." He waved his finger between them. "Yeah, I'm pretty sure he's pissed about that."

She ignored the implication and cockiness of the gesture. "What do you mean, you're pretty sure he's pissed? You haven't talked to him?"

He laughed. "Um. No. I'm not an idiot. I'm staying at his place but I do my best to not be there when he's there because something tells me he won't care that it was you who kissed me."

"I didn't—"

"You did."

She backed off. She couldn't argue, but the fact that he was so cocky about it just pissed her off. "It was a mistake."

"I don't think it was."

"Marcus, it's not like that with you anymore."

"Isn't it?" There was that look again. "I heard you broke up with Malcolm. Because of the kiss? Because of me?"

"What? No. I mean, yes. I mean..." She took a deep breath and worked to compose herself. She would not let Marcus mess with her head. "Yes, I broke up with him. Sort of. We're taking a break."

"Like Ross and Rachel?"

"Who?"

"In *Friends*, the TV show?" He raised an eyebrow.

"Right, whatever. Like that. But we didn't break up."

"Whatever you say." He grinned and she had the distinct

urge to smack it off his face. "But your *break* or whatever, it's because of me, and I think we should probably—"

"No." She held up her hands, needing to put some space between them. "It's not because of you; it's because—"

She stopped herself. She was not about to confide in him. Not about this.

Marcus took her hands in his and held her tight, pinning her with his eyes. "Look. I'm not trying to be a jerk." The change in his voice led her to believe that might be true. "I know I made mistakes with you in the past and I know there's something going on with you and Malcolm, but I also know that we deserve to give this a chance and maybe this is the right time to do that."

"This?"

"Us."

"Us?"

"Kylie, focus."

"There is no us, Marcus."

"There could be."

She shook her head.

"You can't tell me that you never think of the way we were together. The way I kissed you. The way you—"

"Marcus. Stop."

"Just remember who kissed who."

"I told you, that wasn't real."

"It was very real." His gaze darkened. "And you know it."

"No. It wasn't. It was a mistake and you were just in the wrong place at—"

Before she could stop him, he pulled her toward him and tried to kiss her. She turned her head at the last moment, and the kiss landed on her cheek. He pulled away, lifted her gloved hands to his mouth and kissed them chastely before he released her. "Think about it, Kylie. This is our chance and I'm not going to waste it."

She stared after him while he replaced his sunglasses and sauntered down the street away from her. Kylie was confused about what had just happened, but mostly, really pissed off. Out of the corner of her eye, she saw Samantha outside of the pub. Perfect. No doubt now she'd want to talk and get all the details about a situation that only got more confusing every day.

Kylie squared back her shoulders and kept walking.

ARCHER PUT a beer down in front of him, and Malcolm nodded in response. It had taken him three days to come down from the mountain and seek out company. Three days that he hid in his office, only eating when Sandra brought him something from the cafeteria next door and only sleeping when he finally couldn't keep his eyes open any longer. He'd slept on the couch in his office, not wanting to go home in case Marcus had been there. He didn't think his twin brother would be so stupid, but on the other hand, he never would have thought Marcus would kiss his woman.

"How're you doing?"

Archer lounged against the bar across from him, his own glass of draft in hand. He wasn't one to pull any punches, and Malcolm didn't have any illusions of his situation staying a secret in a town like Cedar Springs. At least not for long.

In response, Malcolm lifted his eyebrows and took a healthy swallow of beer. "I'm here."

"That's a good thing. I was going to give you one more day before I came up looking for you."

"I'll be fine."

"I'm sure you will."

The two men drank their beers in silence for a minute. Malcolm knew Archer waited for him to say something. He also knew Archer would wait all day. Finally he asked, "You know the details?"

"I know enough." Archer nodded. "Word gets around."

"Ha." He chuckled, but it wasn't funny.

"So what are you going to do about it?"

And there it was. The question Malcolm had been waiting for. The very same question he'd asked himself for three days. The same question he was no closer to an answer to. He shrugged.

"Really?"

"Really what?" Malcolm put his beer down. "Like I'm supposed to know what the hell to do? She left me, man. For my brother."

"That's bullshit and you know it."

He did. But the fact that it was Marcus Kylie had kissed wasn't an image he could get out of his head. It haunted him.

"Besides that, she didn't leave you. From what I hear, it's a break, so maybe you should stop sitting there feeling sorry for yourself and do something to see about ending that break. And from what I can see, this has nothing to do with your brother."

Malcolm looked up, ready to lash out at his friend. What the hell did Archer know about anything, anyway? All he knew was whatever he'd heard from the locals, who no doubt came into that very bar and gossiped about him. He shook his head; given that fact, Archer probably knew a hell of a lot more than he did.

"But she kissed him."

Archer cocked his head. "Maybe wrong place, right time. I know it's a sore spot for you, but look past your brother and listen to Kylie. What did she tell you?"

Look past his brother. Archer didn't know what he was asking. Of course Marcus was a sore spot with him. He'd had her first. *And he'd lost her.* The voice of reason piped up. Of course, Malcolm was going to lose her, too, if he didn't smarten up. Maybe Archer was right?

"She told me she needed space," Malcolm confessed after a moment. "She told me she doesn't want me to take care of her. What the hell does that even mean? Of course I want to take care of her—I love her."

"What else did she say?"

"Didn't the gossip mill tell you already?" he snapped and took another swallow of beer, wiping his mouth with the back of his hand.

Archer shrugged. "You tell me."

Malcolm paused and relived the conversation in his head again, the same thing he'd been doing for days. "She said she wasn't good enough for me and I'd only ever see her as a waitress."

"Is that true?"

"What?" He slammed his mug down. "No. Hell no."

Archer didn't say anything; he just stared at Malcolm for a moment before he turned away and pulled a fresh pint for him.

"I don't think of her like that," he said after a moment. "She's so much more. She could be so much more."

"But what if she isn't? Is what she is good enough for you? Right now?"

His first instinct was to protest. Of course it was good enough for him. Kylie was perfect exactly the way she was, but he saw so much potential in her. She could be…damn.

"Did I do this?" He ran a hand through his hair and down his face on the scruff that had grown and he hadn't bothered to shave. "Does she think she isn't good enough for me? Is that what all this is?"

Archer shrugged again. "You're going to have to ask her. But if you ask me, I'd say you need to stop dwelling on the fact that your brother happened to show up at the worst time, and do something about getting Kylie back. Have you talked to her? Have you called her?"

He shook his head. He hadn't done any of those things. He'd been way too wounded, hiding away. Sometimes it was just easier to work and hope things would all work out.

But how had that worked for him? Not at all.

"Dammit."

"I'm pretty sure that answers my question." Archer chuckled. "Well, maybe you can ask her later. Stick around—her shift starts soon."

Of course, he knew that already. It was part of the reason he'd finally chosen that afternoon to venture down to the Grizzly Paw. Her work schedule had been written into his calendar in his office in pink pen. It was something she'd started to do a few months ago as a joke, so they'd both know each other's schedules. He'd spent the last few days studying it. Something he'd never bothered to do before.

The door opened and let in a rush of cold air. He turned in his seat, hoping to see Kylie, but it was Samantha who walked in. Disappointed, he turned around before she could see him and returned his focus to his beer and what on earth he was going to do to fix things with Kylie. He vaguely heard Samantha talk to Archer, but he didn't pay any attention. He had more important things to think about.

If it was true that she thought he was disappointed in who and what she was, nothing could be further from the truth, and he needed to make her see that. He'd do his damnedest to convince her that he loved her exactly the way she was. And he could do that. Maybe Archer was right and it had nothing to do with Marcus after all? Maybe it was time for him to swallow his pride and focus on the things that mattered.

"Thank God they made up." Sam's voice pierced his awareness, but still he didn't pay much attention to what most certainly was gossip.

"Who made up?"

"Kylie and Malcolm. Who else?" The mention of his name brought him full force into the conversation. Malcolm sat up and turned to where Sam stood, her back to him, a stack of menus in her hands. "I saw them on Main Street," she said. "And they looked pretty cozy, so I guess whatever they were fighting about is all better and it's about—"

She must have seen the look on Archer's face, or his not so discreet nod, but whatever it was that cued her, Sam turned and saw Malcolm at the bar. He must have looked as if he'd been smacked across the face, because that was certainly how he felt.

"Malcolm."

He nodded.

"I didn't see you there."

"So I gathered."

"So it was…"

"Marcus." He couldn't sit there for another second. He pushed up from the stool and threw some bills on the counter.

"Malcolm." Archer called after him but he didn't turn around. He heard Sam mutter something about how alike they looked and how she wasn't used to having them both in town, but he still didn't stop. He needed air.

If Kylie was getting cozy with Marcus, Archer was wrong. Maybe it was about Marcus.

SHE STILL HAD thirty minutes before her shift started, and she could go into the general store to say hi to Cynthia the way she'd planned, but that was before Marcus had tried to kiss her. The last thing she wanted to do was discuss whatever it was that had just happened with Cynthia. Not yet. Not when she still had no idea what it meant and how she felt about it.

No. She knew how she felt about it.

Things with Marcus had been over long ago, and even if they weren't, it wasn't fair to Malcolm to even think about his brother. Not when they still had so much to figure out. Kissing Marcus on New Year's had just been a mistake: a terrible, champagne-induced mistake that never should have happened.

She needed to clear her head. Instead of turning and walking up the steps to the Grizzly Paw, Kylie kept walking until she hit the end of the road and stepped onto the beach that was covered in snow. In the winter, the town maintained a large skating rink right off the public beach, on the frozen lake. Hay bales had been scattered around for sitting and putting on skates, and on the weekends, they'd light the bonfire and people would gather for hot chocolate and skating with their friends.

There were a few people, kids mostly skating, but it was the man who sat on one of the farthest hay bales, staring out at the lake, who drew her eye. She slid carefully in her boots across the ice, to the far end, where the snow wasn't cleared. She stopped herself from reaching out and touching him.

"Aren't you cold?"

Malcolm turned to look at her. He didn't seem surprised to see her, as if he'd known she'd come. His eyes were tired, as though he hadn't slept much. He most certainly hadn't shaved. She'd never seen him with a scruff on his face. It was sexy and she stuffed her hands in her coat pockets to keep from touching it.

"It's not that bad." His eyes held hers.

"Can I sit?"

"Don't you have to work?"

He knew her schedule? She didn't actually think he looked at the notes she made on his calendar. She shrugged. "Not for a bit."

He turned away, but slid over to make space for her. It

wasn't a large hay bale, which never would have mattered in the past as she would have used it as an excuse to cuddle up with Malcolm and let him wrap his big arm around her and pull her in close. Now, the space seemed excruciatingly small as she perched on the edge, trying not to touch him.

"How've you been?"

It was Malcolm who spoke first.

"Good," she said, out of reflex.

He nodded. "That's good. I'm glad. You deserve to be happy."

Something in his voice scared her. "Malcolm?"

"All I've ever wanted is for you to be happy, Kylie." She turned to look at him, but he stared out onto the ice in front of him. "He won't make you happy. He never did."

His words hit her like a force to the chest. "What? Who?" She asked, but she knew the answer. Marcus.

"I know it's up to me to show you," he continued, as if he hadn't heard her. "And I will, if you give me the chance. But first I need to know one thing." He turned then and looked directly into her eyes.

She nodded slightly, unable to speak.

"I need to know if it's Marcus you want?" He held up a finger when she opened her mouth to protest. "You don't have to answer right away. Think about it." His voice was so calm and controlled it sent a shiver through her. "But I won't compete with my brother, Kylie. I can't."

She shook her head, in as much an effort to clear it as to disagree with him. "It's not like that. This isn't about Marcus. It's about us. About...me."

He stood and brushed his gloved hands down his black wool coat. "If that's true, then what I said before stands. I'll show you exactly how much you mean to me and why you belong with me." The commanding tone to his words sparked something deep inside her and warmed her despite the chill in the air. "Let me know."

He turned to walk away, and by instinct, she reached out to stop him. "I meant what I said." Her voice broke, but he didn't turn around. "This isn't about Marcus." She dropped her hand and Malcolm stood, unmoving.

When he spoke again, his voice was quiet, but hard. "Okay, I believe you."

He made his way across the ice without looking back; Kylie watched him go until he was on the sidewalk, past the Grizzly Paw and completely out of sight.

A sob built up in her chest, and she dropped her face into her gloved hands, releasing the emotions she'd managed to stuff down for the last few days. It was her choice to take a break from their relationship and for what reason? She didn't want to explore things with Marcus, did she?

No.

She could say with certainty, that no, she did not want to explore anything with Marcus.

They had problems before Marcus had come back to town; it was just unfortunate timing. But Malcolm was right; if what she said was true, she couldn't let Marcus confuse her.

She took another minute to pull herself together and wipe her eyes. Her shift started in ten minutes and even though it wouldn't matter one bit if she was late, she made her way quickly across the ice.

He'd said he believed her, but did he? She needed to make things perfectly clear.

She paused before she walked up the steps into the bar. She pulled out her cell phone and sent a text.

I meant what I said. It has nothing to do with Marcus. It never did.

She hit Send and waited. Seconds later, her phone beeped in response.

I told you I believed you and I meant it.

She stood on the sidewalk and waited for him to send something else but her phone remained dark and silent. He'd said he was going to prove to her that she was meant to be with him. Maybe that was true, and maybe he had something in mind, but whatever it was that Malcolm planned, she had plans of her own and they involved looking after herself. Kylie stuffed her phone back into her pocket and with a newfound resolve, walked into the Grizzly Paw. She was done waiting for life to happen to her.

Chapter Seven

SHE DIDN'T HEAR from Malcolm later that day, or the next morning. By the following afternoon, she had started to go a little stir crazy, and was almost ready to drive up to the ski hill and confront him. Almost. She still had her own life to worry about and that's exactly what she had been doing for the last twenty-four hours: worrying.

The scent coming off the freshly baked cinnamon bun in front of her made her mouth water, but she'd told herself she wouldn't touch it until she'd finished filling out the paperwork in front of her. She'd already completed all the easy questions, like date of birth and address. It was the other questions on the application form that stopped her. Questions like... *What makes you a qualified applicant for our program? And, What qualities do you possess that would make you a good nurse?*

She'd stared at those questions for hours and had somehow thought that the enticement of one of Suzy Crosswell's famous cinnamon buns from Dream Puffs would make them easier to answer. With a deep breath, she picked up her pen and filled in the blanks of the first question. She let the pen move across the page and tried not to overthink her answer, deciding an honest answer from the heart would be best. She was so focused that she hadn't even heard the bells over the bakery door jangle, nor did she notice her best friend until she was directly in front of her.

"Is it true?"

Startled, Kylie sat up and instinctively pulled the paper toward her so her friend couldn't see. "What?"

"Did you quit your job without telling me?"

"Oh, that." She nodded. "I guess I did."

"You guess you did?" Cynthia sat back in the chair and shook her head. "How did that slip your mind? What happened? What are you going to do? When did you decide to do that? What—"

"Stop." Kylie laughed and held up her hand to stop Cynthia's interrogation.

Cynthia shook her head; her red hair swished over her shoulders. "What is wrong with you? You think it's funny? I don't get it. You've worked at the Paw forever."

"I know." That was the problem, but she didn't expect Cynthia to see that logic. At least not right away. "It was time for a change."

"So what are you going to be doing? I still don't know everything that happened with you and Malcolm, but you guys aren't back together, are you? Wait!" She sat up straight in her chair and a smile crossed her face. "That's it, isn't it? You're back together and getting married and that's why you don't need to work anymore. I'm right, aren't I?"

Kylie pulled the pastry toward her and ripped off a chunk. It was clear that she wasn't going to be able to fill out her form any time soon, so she might as well eat it while it was fresh. "That's not it. And why do you think I don't need to work if I'm with Malcolm?" The idea that even her best friend thought that pissed her off a little. More than a little.

"Hold that thought," Cynthia said. "I'm going to grab a coffee."

She used the time to try to figure out what she was going to tell Cynthia, but when her friend returned, she was no closer to an explanation, aside from the truth. And she wasn't totally sure she was ready for that.

"So." Cynthia sat down across from Kylie again. "Spill. What the hell is going on with you? You've been acting crazy for weeks and everything at New Year's…well, that was just crazy on top of crazy."

Kylie opened her mouth to say something, but Cynthia cut her off. "And I know you're not telling me everything about what went down at the party, but I know something big happened and don't think I'm not a little hurt that I had to hear from Melanie Braid that you kissed Marcus at the party. I'm your best friend, for goodness' sake—shouldn't I be the first to know these things? Well, besides Malcolm, of course. Oh my God. Is that it? Is that why you broke up? Did Malcolm lose his shit that you kissed his brother? Because I can—"

"Would you please stop it? Seriously." Kylie's head spun with all of Cynthia's talking. She was surprised that Cynthia had heard about the kiss from Melanie. She wasn't usually the gossipy type, but maybe the New Year's incident—as she was coming to think of it—was newsworthy for even the best secret keeper. She took another sip of her coffee. So much for thinking no one had seen it. Not that she really believed she could keep it a secret for long. But still.

Cynthia sat across the table from her, a frown on her face. She was hurt. Of course she was. Kylie had been a shitty friend. She'd add it to the list of things she'd screwed up at lately. But at least this was one thing she might have a shot at fixing. She reached across the table and squeezed Cynthia's hand. "I'm sorry," she said. "It's not that I didn't want to tell you what happened; I just didn't know how to explain everything when I don't even understand it myself."

"You could try."

"I could." Kylie nodded. "And I will."

Because it was what her friend deserved from her and Kylie was finally ready to talk, she spent the next twenty minutes filling Cynthia in on everything, starting before the New Year's party and her restlessness with her relationship. When she had finished, she crammed the rest of the cinnamon bun in her mouth and took her time chewing.

Cynthia, who'd been quiet the entire time she spoke, nodded and smiled. "So that's it? You're not sure what you want to be when you grow up, so you broke up with Malcolm and made him think it's because of his twin brother?"

Kylie almost choked and grabbed her now cold coffee to try to swallow down the bun. When she was adequately recovered, she swallowed and said, "No. It's not like that at all."

"Sounds like that's exactly what it's like. You're being an idiot."

"Thanks a lot." Maybe she'd made a mistake confiding in her friend after all.

Cynthia waved her hand to dismiss Kylie's sarcasm. "Seriously, Kylie. Stop and think about it. You have this great guy who wants to give you the world, and you totally sabotaged it the best way you could. I mean, even if you didn't want to tell him about your dreams and goals, you didn't have to do what you did. And his brother? If I didn't know better, I'd think that you went out of your way to screw this up."

"It's not like that," she protested, but Kylie couldn't come up with the energy to be really angry. "Not really," she finished weakly.

"It's okay, Kylie. I get it." Cynthia smiled sympathetically, giving Kylie an ounce of hope that she wasn't totally alone in all this. "You were scared and you freaked out."

"I don't want to be my mother."

Cynthia laughed. "As if you could. You are nothing like your mother. You're too much like your father." She winked.

"I'm afraid of that, too." Kylie laughed a little, too.

"Maybe it's time to stop being so afraid of who you aren't, and start figuring out who you are."

"Wow, Cyn. That's pretty profound, especially for you."

For a second, Kylie thought her friend would object to the friendly insult; instead, she laughed. "I know, right?"

HE SHOULD HAVE BEEN GOING over ticket sales numbers and the latest snow reports that Seth had given him. At the very least, Malcolm should have been thinking about what sites to use for the photo shoot Bria Sheridan was going to do for Stone Summit. Hell, Malcolm could have been doing any number of things on his to-do list, but none of them were important. At least not as important as the one project he was working on.

Project Kylie.

It wasn't so much a project, really, as a mission. After hearing about how she'd been spotted kissing Marcus again, something snapped in him. His initial reaction had been to lash out, find his brother and beat him to a pulp. But as much as that might have made him feel good in the short term, Malcolm wasn't stupid enough to follow through on it. Not in a small town where everyone knew everyone and he had a business to run. Besides, he was better than that.

So he'd gone out onto the ice instead and when he'd seen Kylie standing over him, it all became clear. He didn't know the details of the kisses, and God help him, he didn't want to know. What he did know was what he had with her and that's what he was going to focus on, because there was no way that she didn't feel the exact same way that he did. No matter what was going on with her, the one thing that was constant was the connection the two of them had, and he needed to remind her of that. It didn't take a genius to figure out that he'd been preoccupied lately. He probably hadn't given her enough attention. But that was going to change. Starting with the first phase of his plan.

He looked down to the notes he'd hastily sketched out. The first thing he needed to do was spend time with her. Lots of time. Just the two of them, doing something no-pressure. Something they both enjoyed.

Skiing.

Malcolm grinned and turned to his computer, where he quickly typed up a letter and hit print. There was only one other part to his plan. He crossed the room and picked up the unique backpack he'd found in the Stone Summit gift shop. He made a mental note to tell Cassidy Langly, his business manager, what a good job she was doing. If she'd selected such unique items for the pro shop besides the usual gloves and hats, it was bound to be a success. Inside, the bag was designed to hold two wine glasses, plates, and napkins. There was room for snacks and a blanket as well. He'd already taken care of the blanket but the rest was up to Kylie. It was all in the letter.

She told him she didn't want to be a kept woman. Damn stubborn woman. As much as he wanted to take care of her and tell her exactly how things were going to go, she had a strong will and dammit if that wasn't one of the things he loved about her. Besides that, it was sexy as hell. Either way, he was determined to let her strong will work in his favor too. He took the letter off the printer, folded it and stuck it inside the bag before he zipped it up.

"Sandra." Malcolm grabbed his coat and made his way to the front office. "I need you to make sure this gets to Kylie right away."

"Kylie?" She lifted her eyebrow and if she wasn't practically like a mother to him, he might have taken exception. The problem was, Sandra knew him too well and she probably knew better than he did what was going on between him and Kylie.

"Yes. I need it delivered to her within the hour. Preferably sooner." He turned before he went out the door. "And it has to be hand delivered. Not left at her door for anyone to pick up."

"Yes sir."

He ignored the sarcasm.

"Anything else, boss?"

"One thing." Malcolm held up a finger and pointed at the bag Sandra held out. "Can you wrap it up or something? A big white box with a red bow maybe?"

"Christmas was two weeks ago."

"I'm aware. Just do it, please."

Sandra smiled and winked at him. For all the guff she dished out, Malcolm knew the woman was totally on his side. "I'll make sure it's delivered. I can't promise fancy wrapping—some of us have work to do."

"You're the best."

"I know."

He pushed the door open and braced himself against the cold air that blasted him in the face, but Sandra's voice stopped him before he stepped outside. "Will you be back? Or can I reach you on your cell if I need to?"

Malcolm turned around. "I won't be back today. I have something to take care of."

"Something involving your brother, I hope."

He blinked hard and stared at her, but Sandra kept a demure smile on her face as if she'd just said the sweetest thing possible. Reluctantly, Malcolm nodded before he walked out. The door closed behind him, but he was certain he heard Sandra say the words, "It's about time," as he walked away.

KYLIE HADN'T BEEN able to finish filling out the application for nursing school in front of Cynthia, but she had managed to stuff it into her purse without her friend noticing. It's not that she didn't want her best friend to know what she was doing, but she didn't really want anyone to know until there was something to know. And at the moment, there was just a whole bunch of questions. Including the big one: *What if I don't get in?* And then the even bigger one: *What if I do get in?*

When she'd walked into the Grizzly Paw the day before, Kylie certainly hadn't planned to quit her job and sure, she probably should have waited until she had a sure thing lined up, or not lined up, as far as nursing school went. After all, even if she did get accepted, classes wouldn't start until spring and if she didn't get in, she'd still need a job. But when she walked in and looked at Archer and Sam, some of her closest friends staring at her as if she would break if the wind blew a certain way, she knew she couldn't keep doing what she was doing. She needed to make a change. And sometimes a change needed to be accompanied by a major there's no turning back type of moment. So she'd sat Samantha down and told her that she had to quit.

To her surprise, Sam hadn't really seemed that surprised. Almost as if she knew Kylie was going to do something drastic. And given that they'd just hired a new girl and it wasn't really all that busy in the middle of winter, Sam was nice enough to pay Kylie out her two weeks instead of making her work it. She knew Sam didn't have to do that; it was a move born out of friendship. Sam knew Kylie needed the time and the money, and she could have kissed her for it.

In fact, she did kiss her. She also gave Archer a big hug and promised them both that she wouldn't be a stranger, as if she could be in such a small town. They all knew she'd be back, but hopefully the next time she walked through the doors of the Grizzly Paw, she'd be on the other side of the counter, enjoying a drink with friends instead of serving them. The thought made her smile.

It made her smile still as she sat at her tiny kitchen table and filled out the rest of her nursing school application. After a bit of time away, the answers came to her easily and she filled them out quickly before she folded the paper and sealed it in an envelope. She needed to eliminate the option of second-guessing herself. She fished a few stamps out of her wallet and grabbed her coat to make the short walk to the post office before she chickened out.

The day was crisp, but not too cold despite the blue sky overhead. Instantly her thoughts went to Malcolm and the ski hill. Did they have enough snow? How were the ticket sales? He'd been so worried about the first season, obsessing over the Farmer's Almanac, trying to predict what the weather would be. Malcolm said if the first season was successful, it would set the hill up for the future, but if they didn't get the snow they needed, it would be hard to convince the skiers to come out to Stone Summit.

Of course she worried; she still cared about Malcolm. No. She still loved him and that was the whole problem. As stupid as their *break* or whatever it was might sound to their friends, Kylie needed it precisely because she did love Malcolm. But she needed to figure out herself before she could give everything to Malcolm.

"Kylie!"

A voice stopped her and she swung around to see Jules, Beth Martin's daughter, running toward her. The girl came to a screeching halt, not in small part because of the icy sidewalk, in front of her. "I'm glad I caught you." Her breath came in short bursts. "I was on my way to your house and then I saw you leave and I thought, oh God if you leave I'll never find you and I was told to give this to you personally and not leave it on your porch. Not that I would have left it on your porch, but sometimes it's easier to—"

"Whoa." Kylie held up her hands to slow the girl down at least long enough so she could catch up. "What are you talking about? You're supposed to deliver something to me?"

Jules pulled a backpack off her shoulder and thrust it into Kylie's arms. "Here. If anyone asks, I gave it to you, okay?"

"You did give it to me."

"I know, but just in case anyone asks, could you maybe say it was wrapped?"

Kylie eyed the girl for a moment. Teenagers were strange and she'd never be able to understand their mixed-up logic. "Wrapped?"

"Yeah, just pretend it was wrapped, okay?"

Kylie tilted her head and narrowed her eyes until Jules added, "I'm sorry. I said I'd wrap it but I couldn't find a bow and...they offered me twenty dollars, so I kinda feel bad, but I wanted to make sure you got it and—"

"It's fine, Jules." Kylie tried not to laugh. "If anyone asks, it was beautifully wrapped. Who is it from?"

"I don't know. I was told to deliver it to you. No exceptions."

"Who told you?"

She shrugged and it was clear Kylie wasn't going to get any more information out of the girl.

"Well, thanks."

"No problem. Are you going to the post office?" She nodded toward the letter Kylie balanced in her hand along with the backpack.

Kylie glanced at the letter in her hand and clutched it to her body possessively. "I am."

"I'm going right past there. I have to meet my mom at the store. I can deliver it for you if you want," she said in the way teenage girls do when they don't really want to appear helpful. "Or whatever."

"You could," Kylie hedged, not sure she wanted to release her application into the world yet. "But I was kind of looking forward to the fresh air and I could use the walk…"

"Whatever. I thought I'd help. No biggie. Besides, aren't you curious about the bag?"

She looked to the bag. Of course she was curious.

"I think there's a letter in the front pocket." Jules held up her hands. "Not that I looked or anything, but it's in an envelope anyway, so…ya know."

Kylie couldn't help but laugh. She shifted the bag and reached into the front pocket. The letter was sealed in a plain envelope with no clue as to who it was from. She slung the pack on her back and opened the letter. After a quick scan, she immediately folded it and tucked it away.

"Well?" Jules peered out from under her slouchy knit cap. "Who's it from?"

It wasn't a question Kylie was ready to answer. Instead, she took a last look at her application letter, sealed and ready to send. She gave it a silent prayer and passed it to Jules. "If it wouldn't be too much trouble, could you put that in the mailbox on your way past? It's all stamped and ready to go, but I should probably get home. I have a few things to do that I forgot about."

From the look on Jules's face, there was no way she was falling for her story, but she grinned and nodded. "No prob."

She turned to leave and Kylie didn't even bother to waste another moment. With a flutter of excitement in her belly, Kylie turned on her heel and headed straight back home so she could read the letter again and follow the instructions written there.

MALCOLM TRIED NOT to think about the gift he'd left in Sandra's hands. There was no doubt that it would be delivered to Kylie. He wasn't worried about that. If Sandra said she was going to do something, she did it. No, he was worried about the response he'd get from Kylie. Would she be excited? Or annoyed?

No. She wouldn't be annoyed. That wasn't Kylie's style. Hopefully she'd be interested enough to take him up on his offer, but he wouldn't know either way until tomorrow afternoon, so there was no point dwelling on it. Especially when he had other things to take care of. Well, one thing in particular. And it certainly wouldn't be nearly as enjoyable, but it was definitely necessary.

It wasn't all that cold, particularly for a January day in the mountains, but he zipped his coat against the wind anyway. The morning had started off bright and sunny, but it was quickly closing in with a thick cloud cover that promised snow. More snow was always a good thing. Stone Summit had enjoyed a good run so far, but there was one thing a ski hill needed to be successful, and that was more snow. Always.

He made the short walk down the wooded path away from the lodge and the ski hill building, toward his chalet. He'd been avoiding home for the last few days, knowing Marcus had to be there at least some of the time, but it was time for that to end. He needed to find his brother, and with any luck, he would.

Sure enough, as Malcolm made his way around the side of his log style home, he noticed the light in the living room on. Marcus was home. He took a deep breath and forced himself to stay calm before he walked in the side door. The sound of the television came from the front room but Malcolm didn't bother to call out or announce himself. It was definitely better to have the element of surprise on his side.

He left his boots at the door and walked through the kitchen, leaving his jacket on the back of a chair. Marcus was sprawled on the couch, his back to him, and he was alone. Not that Malcolm really expected him to have a woman in the house, not if he was after Kylie, but then again, it was Marcus.

As soon as there was a lull in the television show he was watching, Malcolm spoke. "We need to talk."

Startled, Marcus scrambled to his feet and turned around. His mouth gaped at Malcolm. "What…you're…what are you doing here?"

"It's my house."

"But shouldn't you be at the hill?"

Malcolm didn't bother to answer. He leaned against the wall and crossed his arms. "That's what you've been doing? Coming here while I'm at work? I guessed as much. But where have you been at night?"

He didn't really want the answer to that question, especially if it involved Kylie, but deep down he knew it didn't. Kylie wouldn't hurt him like that. The image of them kissing flashed through his head, but he pushed it away before it could take root. Marcus's mind must have gone to the same place because a grin slid across his face. It quickly disappeared when Malcolm stood straight and flexed his fingers into a fist.

"It's not like that." Marcus held up his hand.

"I know." Even if he wasn't totally confident, he needed to present himself that way, at least to his brother. "You're stupid, but you're not that stupid."

Marcus opened his mouth to say something, but closed it again and ran a hand over his face. "Look, I don't want to fight with you, Malc. It's been too long, and you're my brother. I don't want anything coming between us, especially not a—"

"Don't say it." He didn't want to, but if Marcus said one derogatory comment toward Kylie, he'd punch him. No questions asked. "Whatever you were about to say about Kylie, think twice."

"I wouldn't say anything bad about her. I...I care about her, too."

It probably would have been better if he'd said something rude. At least with that, Malcolm would know how to react. He did not know how to deal with what Marcus had just said. He turned away, lest something show on his face, and took the moment to compose himself. Finally, he shook his head and turned back. "No," he said. "You gave up the right to care about her a long time ago. That's over. This isn't about you."

"It is."

"No," he said, stronger this time, remembering the words Kylie had texted him. *It has nothing to do with Marcus.* "It's not." He had to believe her. If there was ever going to be a future with them, he had to believe what she said. And he did.

"I know it's not about me, not really." Marcus shook his head. "But I still care about her. You need to know that."

Malcolm shook his head. "You don't want to tell me that right now."

"I have to."

Malcolm's fingers twitched, itching to lash out at his brother.

"Kylie was the only woman I could have had something real with. She was the only one who accepted me, and tried to know me. I screwed up with her."

If Malcolm hadn't been so angry, he might have felt a little bit sorry for his brother. Might have. The truth was, Marcus had created his reality with his actions. "You did. Now live with it."

"I don't think I can do that." Marcus's face hardened. "I need to know."

He was almost positive he wasn't going to like what he was about to hear, but he asked the question anyway. "What do you need to know?"

"If she still has feelings for me."

He was right. He didn't want to hear it, and at his brother's words, Malcolm's vision went black. There was no way this was going to happen. He shook his head, not trusting himself to speak.

"You know I'm right, Malcolm. You have to admit that there's at least part of you that's always wondered the same thing."

No.

"You can't tell me that you've never wondered if Kylie still has feelings for me. After all, I was first."

That was it. Malcolm took two steps forward, crossed the distance between them and swung his fist. It should have connected, but Marcus had grown up fighting with his brother and he dodged the punch easily.

"Do it," Marcus said. "Try to hit me." Malcolm charged him, connecting solidly with his brother and knocking him to the wood floor. They scuffled, each brother trying to get the upper hand. As identical twins, they'd always been an even match as far as wrestling, but time had created changes in each of them and now Malcolm was strong, his muscles honed from hours in the gym, but Marcus was fit, too. His wiry strength made him fast and an able opponent. They each got in a few hits before finally, Malcolm pinned Marcus beneath him.

Knowing he'd been caught, Marcus tilted his head and looked directly at his brother. "Hit me. Will that make you feel better? Hit me then."

His breath heaving, Malcolm held his fist aloft, ready to make contact with a face eerily similar to his own. It might make him feel better. God knew he needed something to ease the stress, but was it punching Marcus?

"Go ahead," Marcus taunted. "Do it. But it's not going to change anything. I know you well enough to know exactly what's going on in your head. You wanted Kylie from day one, but she chose me and that made you crazy. The only reason you had her at all is because I left."

His brother's words stung, and he knew it.

"And you've always wondered *what if*, haven't you?"

Malcolm growled in response. His brother was way too close to the mark. He raised his fist higher again.

"Hit me." Marcus looked straight at him, and Malcolm stared down into the same blue eyes as if he looked in a mirror.

Damn it.

He rolled off his brother, and sat next to him, his arms around his knees. Marcus pulled himself up to sitting and adopted an identical position, so they faced each other. Malcolm had forgotten how alike they really were.

But not in everything.

They stared at each other in silence for a few moments. There was truth in what Marcus said, and that pissed him off. Of course he'd wondered about Kylie's feelings. He'd watched for too long as Marcus treated her poorly, and she stayed with him, believing he was her true love. It had taken years for him to work up the courage to finally tell her how he felt about her: that it was him, not his brother, who'd done all the sweet things she'd held on to as Marcus continually betrayed their relationship. It had taken a long time, but Malcolm had never given up hope that he'd one day have her and she'd feel the same way about him. And then, she did. He remembered those days on the island of Eden, where he finally saw the look in her eyes that he'd dreamt about. She did love him. Malcolm. But that hadn't prevented him from questioning it, and Marcus was smart enough to know it.

"Fine," Malcolm said after a moment. "You think she still cares about you? I'm not going to stop you from trying to see if that's true." He couldn't believe the words were coming out of his mouth, but he held on to what Kylie had said. *It has nothing to do with Marcus.* He trusted her and more than that, he trusted what they had. They might be on a break or whatever she wanted to call it, but he was confident he could overcome it. What he had with Kylie was a million times stronger than anything Marcus had ever had with her. It was real.

"Really?"

Malcolm nodded. "But then it's over. I'm not doing this anymore. Whatever she decides, either way. That's it. We're brothers, and that will never change."

Marcus mulled it over, and then nodded the way Malcolm knew he would. "Deal." He reached forward and extended his hand, which Malcolm took and pulled him into a hug, complete with back slaps.

When he pulled himself up to his feet, and dusted off his jeans, he turned to Marcus, who'd done the same. "I'm glad to have you here. Despite everything. I missed you."

"Me too." Marcus nodded. "Me too."

It was about as mushy as they ever got, and he'd had enough. Malcolm headed to the kitchen to grab them each a cold beer. Before he got there, he turned and added, "But you're going to need to move out."

"What?"

"Yup." Malcolm smiled. "I love you, Marc. But you're going to cramp my style if you stick around here. I'll help you find something." He passed his twin a beer. "After we hit the slopes. I haven't had the chance to properly show off my hill yet."

They clinked bottles and took healthy swallows of their beers. The relationship between twin brothers was complicated, especially when a woman was involved, but regardless how it all turned out, Marcus would always be his brother.

Besides, Malcolm thought with a wry smile, after tomorrow, if Kylie followed the instructions in his letter, there would be no doubt how she felt.

Chapter Eight

KYLIE WATCHED the skiers and snowboarders swishing their way down the slopes beneath her as she rode the chairlift to the top of the mountain and where Malcolm should be waiting for her. Should be. Of course he would be. He'd sent the letter and the backpack. She looked to the seat next to her where the backpack, full of the supplies she'd packed, rested.

A smile crossed her lips. There'd been a certain tone to Malcolm's letter. Something she couldn't quite pinpoint, but it had been more commanding than usual. As though it wasn't a request that she meet him, but more of an expectation. She couldn't help it; the idea thrilled her. She missed him. And even if she wasn't any closer to figuring out her own future, she'd taken steps, and she wanted to share them with Malcolm.

The chairlift crested the hill and she could see the little house at the top, which meant she was almost there. Her stomach flipped with expectation, which was ridiculous, because after all, it was Malcolm. They'd done this before. It's not as if it were their first date. But there was pressure on it, and wasn't that why she changed her outfit three times before she decided on a blue sweater and black leggings to wear under her ski clothes? Not like it mattered anyway, since from the sounds of the letter, they'd only be skiing together.

They'd also be sharing a bottle of wine and a selection of cheese and crackers that Kylie had picked up and packed, along with the glasses and blanket that were already in the bag.

Not that she had any idea where they'd be enjoying the wine in the middle of the ski hill. "Just go with it," she told herself for the dozenth time. She really needed to learn how to just relax and go with the flow instead of work herself up over every little detail.

Just like on the island, she reminded herself. When Malcolm had sent her the invitation to the island of Eden, she'd thrown all her hesitations aside and totally allowed herself to be open to anything and everything. And that's how she'd realized that it was always Malcolm she loved, not Marcus.

Not Marcus.

She touched her gloved fingers to her lips, remembering the way he'd kissed her. She told him there was nothing between them and she'd meant it. At least she thought she had. Why did doubts have to creep in now? She shook her head to clear it. No. Just because things were rocky with Malcolm at the moment didn't mean anything. She'd told Malcolm it had nothing to do with Marcus, and she needed to remember that.

The chair grew closer to the dismount area, and Kylie flipped the safety bar up and picked up the backpack in her free hand; her other hand held her poles. As her skis hit the snow beneath her, she pushed off and skied away from the lift. After a quick scan of the people standing at the top of the hill, she couldn't see Malcolm. She checked the large clock that was mounted atop the map of the ski runs. She was right on time.

"Kylie?"

She turned and there he was, looking extremely sexy in his ski jacket and helmet. He still hadn't shaved the scruff on his cheeks and damn, it was sexy.

"You came."

"Did you doubt me?"

He smiled and reached out with his gloved hand and touched one finger to her cheek, which was incredibly intimate, despite the ski gear separating them. "Not for a second," he said. "I trust you followed the instructions?" He gestured to the backpack and another thrill went through her at the commanding tone in his voice. She'd always loved it when he took charge.

Just not when he took over, a little voice in her head reminded her. That's what their break, or whatever it was, was all about. She needed to remember that.

"Don't trust me." She grinned and thrust the bag toward him. "Check for yourself."

His eyebrows lifted a little. "It's going to be like that, is it?" He laughed. "Okay, then. Think you can keep up?"

It was the right thing to say, and he knew it. Skiing had always been the area where both of them were equal. When they were younger, they'd race, each pushing the other to go farther, faster, take bigger risks. It had been a powerful turn-on. Only back then, it was Marcus she turned to for the sexual release the activity built in her.

Since they'd been together, they'd only been skiing together a few times, and both times it had been mild, sticking to the groomed runs, checking on the snow conditions and the operations. It had been business.

This was going to be fun.

She winked at him, and planted her poles, ready to push off. "Try to keep up with me."

Kylie pushed off hard and cut a line down the easy groomed run, with absolutely no intention to stay there. She knew she had an unfair advantage, considering Malcolm had the pack, and when she'd taken off, he was still holding it, but

Malcolm was strong and she had no doubt he'd be right behind her.

Sure enough, it wasn't long before she heard the sounds of his skis cutting close to her. It was time. With a sharp turn to the left, Kylie cut into the trees, leaving the safe, groomed run behind. In the trees, the snow was softer, deeper, and way more fun. Every time she planted her pole, Kylie pushed herself harder, sinking into the turns, her quads squatting deep and burning up with the familiar heat of muscle exertion. She lost herself to the rhythm of the precise turns as she cut her way through the forest. Soon there was a flash of green on her right.

Malcolm.

She didn't let him distract her; instead, she kept her gaze slightly forward, looking for the next turn, and then the next until finally she'd cleared the trees. She came to a stop with a flurry of snow flying behind her only moments before Malcolm did the same thing directly in front of her.

NEITHER OF THEM SPOKE. They were too busy catching their breath. After a moment, Malcolm lifted his head and tugged his goggles up over his helmet.

"Damn." Was all he said.

"Right back at ya."

In that moment, looking at the smile on Kylie's gorgeous face, her long dark braid falling over her shoulder, looking sexy as sin in her tight ski pants, he knew he'd made the right decision by getting her out on the hill.

"It's been years since we've done that."

She nodded, her eyes darkening momentarily. "Let's do it again."

He couldn't refuse that. Besides, the rest of his plan could wait. "As you wish, babe."

They made two more trips up the chairlift, laughing and talking easily, and once they were back on the hill, they pushed hard down the run as they drove each other to the very limits of what they could do. There was no doubt they both could keep going, but Malcolm was getting restless. It was time to move on.

When they got to the top of the chair again, both skiing off and getting into position, Malcolm stopped Kylie with a hand on her arm. "This time, follow me. I have a surprise."

He didn't wait for a response, but skied away knowing she'd follow. The pace was slightly slower, but only because he didn't want to miss his turnoff. Kylie was right behind him, and when he made the turn, she made it too and he could have sworn he heard her say something. He smiled, knowing what it probably was.

They took a tight trail that didn't allow for much turning, only trusting that nothing would go wrong as they both picked up speed through the trees. They were going so quickly on the tight packed trail that if anyone caught an edge, or lost focus, it would mean a messy spill. It had never happened before, but the last time they were on the track, they'd been a lot younger. Things had been different, and Malcolm couldn't help but wonder whether Kylie remembered the trail. She'd remember.

Right as the speed almost became too much, the trail opened up into a clearing with a small wooden house tucked into the far edge. It almost blended in with the trees, it was so small and rustic. Almost, but not quite.

Without bothering to look behind him, Malcolm pushed forward on his skis until he was in front of the cabin. It wasn't until he clicked out of his skis and picked them up, leaning them against the rough wood, that he turned around.

The look on Kylie's face told him everything he needed to know. She was surprised. More than surprised.

She had pushed her way to the cabin, but still stood in her skis. Her hand was over her mouth and Malcolm couldn't be sure, but there almost looked to be tears in her eyes. With a grin he never wanted to wipe off on his face, he strode over to her. "Do you remember this place?"

She nodded. "But it was…"

"Abandoned?" He nodded. "Not anymore. Come on, I'll show you."

Kylie used her poles to click out of her skis, and Malcolm bent down to pick them up and leave them next to his. He took her hand and led her to the front door of the shack. No doubt she was confused. When they were barely more than kids, and they thought they ran the ski hill, they'd discovered the abandoned little hut one day. Marcus hadn't come out with them that day, begging off due to a sore calf muscle. But Malcolm knew the truth. His brother had been meeting up with some girl, cheating on Kylie again. He'd kept quiet then, although when they'd stumbled upon the abandoned cabin and gone inside, building a fire, just because they could, he almost told her. It would have been easy to confess his brother's sins, but it wouldn't have been the right time.

Besides that, they'd always kept the discovery of the cabin a secret. He'd always expected Kylie to tell Marcus, but she hadn't, and it had always been their secret. They'd only escaped one other time to their secret spot, and Malcolm had almost kissed her, but the moment passed and he swore the next time he got her alone at the cabin, he would. But he never got the chance, because right after that, Marcus had taken the offer to go pro, leaving Cedar Springs, and Kylie, behind. Malcolm had left for school shortly after that. He refused to be her rebound and he needed to bide his time. Which he had.

But now they were back, and things were different. Very different.

He took off his gloves, reached into his pocket and withdrew a key.

"It was never locked before."

"That was before." He unlocked the door and pushed it open for her to go in first.

She hesitated. "Are you sure it's okay? I mean, it's not trespassing?"

He couldn't help it; he laughed. "Kylie, I own it. It's part of the hill. Besides, trespassing never stopped you before."

She wrinkled her nose at him and walked in.

IT WAS SO DIFFERENT, yet totally the same. Kylie took her time taking in the little hut—and it was little. Just four simple walls with a fireplace at one end. A large trunk sat under the only window and two chairs were pushed up against the other wall, flanking the door. When they'd discovered the little hut there was no furniture at all. Just an empty shell, and a roof that was almost falling in. The chimney had been blocked by a nest or something, which they'd discovered when they tried to build a fire and it had smoked them out. Not to be deterred, they'd built the fire outside, just outside the front door.

She couldn't remember why now that it was so important that they get the fire going, but they'd both been so determined and so proud of themselves when finally they'd accomplished it.

Now there was a pile of wood next to the fireplace, and Kylie knew without asking, the chimney was clear. Someone had definitely put some time and attention into the little place. She couldn't believe she'd forgotten all about it.

"You did this?"

Malcolm nodded and removed his helmet. He ran a hand through his hair. "I did. I have a lot of fond memories from this place."

She nodded and looked around again. "Me too." It was true. She may not have been dating Malcolm back then, but hanging out with him, talking, and just being…real—something she couldn't seem to do with Marcus—they had been some of her fondest memories. "Me too," she whispered. "I can't believe you didn't tell me you did this."

"I wanted it to be a surprise for Valentine's Day."

"Valentine's Day?"

He nodded and gently unclipped her helmet, removing it before he slid the back of one finger down her cheek. The intimate gesture felt both familiar and completely new at the same time. She shivered, a spark lighting her core and the desire that had built up from their hard skiing.

"It was the day we discovered this place, remember?"

She did. It all came back to her. Marcus had a sore leg or something, so they'd gone out without him and when they'd returned, she'd naively thought Marcus would have planned something for them for Valentine's Day, but instead she couldn't get a hold of him. Nobody had seen him, or at least that's what they told her. He didn't turn up until the next day. She knew now what she probably should have figured out back then. He was with another woman. She shook her head. It didn't matter now, anyway, except to cement the idea in her head that whatever was going on with her, it had nothing to do with Marcus.

She turned and looked in Malcolm's eyes. "You did this for me?"

"For us."

She shivered, but it wasn't because of the cold.

"Let me make a fire." Malcolm released her. "You're cold."

"I'm…" She let her objection drift away because at that

moment she wanted nothing more than to sit by the fire with Malcolm in *their* cabin. While Malcolm gathered the supplies that he'd obviously prepared in advance, Kylie walked around the tiny space and took in every detail. He'd done this for her, because it had meant something to him. Because she meant something to him.

"So?"

Kylie turned at the sound of Malcolm's voice. The fire was crackling to life in the hearth and Malcolm had moved so he was directly behind her. Despite thick jackets between them, she could feel the heat coming from him. Or maybe that was just her and the way her body responded to him. That hadn't changed between them. She was still intensely attracted to him.

"What do you think? Do you like it?"

"I love it." She took his hand, but immediately dropped it, not sure if that kind of contact between them was okay when they were on a break. "I'm sorry I ruined your Valentine's Day surprise." She looked up at his eyes, not able to look at his hand that she so badly wanted back in hers.

"This is better." His voice was soft, but his eyes were anything but as they bored into hers. He took a step toward her, closed the distance between them so they were just a fraction of an inch apart. "It's okay to touch me, you know?" She swallowed hard at the way he could read her mind. "If you want to, that is."

He knew damn well she wanted to touch him. She wanted to feel the heat from his skin on hers. She wanted his arms wrapped around her; she wanted his lips on hers. She wanted it all.

She also wanted space between them. She wanted him to understand how she felt.

Damn it.

Kylie turned away moments before she reached for him. She didn't know what she wanted. It was too much.

"Kylie, it doesn't have to be like this."

She nodded, unable to look at him. "It does. At least for now."

She expected him to protest, to argue his point and push it. Instead, he did the exact opposite. "Okay." She felt him move away, or more accurately, she felt the cold space behind her.

Kylie turned and stared at him, openmouthed. Malcolm never gave up so easily.

"I respect you, babe. I know you need to figure stuff out and while I don't like it, I respect it." He looked genuine, and she had no reason to think otherwise.

"Okay," she said cautiously. "Thanks."

His face lit up in a sexy smile that caused her stomach to flip a little. "Why don't you come and enjoy the fire with me, at least. If that's okay?"

IT HAD TAKEN ALL the self-control he had not to put his hands on her, pull her close and kiss all the indecision out of her. Somehow he'd managed to pull it together. If she wanted a break, he'd give it to her, but he also had every intention to make it very difficult for her to resist breaking her own rules.

The cabin had been perfectly prepared for this moment. He went to the trunk and pulled out a stack of thick, soft blankets that he laid out in front of the fire.

"It's getting warm in here." He took his jacket off and motioned for her to do the same. "Take your jacket off, Kylie, and maybe your ski boots, too. Why not get comfortable?"

She eyed him suspiciously, no doubt assuming he had some ulterior motive, which he did, but she didn't need to know that.

"That probably makes sense," she said, but didn't move to take her ski clothes off.

"Kylie, I'm not going to bite. It's me. Besides, I told you I respect your decision for a break. Whatever it is you need, babe. I get it. I'm not suggesting we get naked or anything." Although, that's what he would have preferred. He glanced away before she could see the want on his face and instead busied himself with removing his heavy ski boots.

It wasn't until he was done that he finally looked back to Kylie and was pleased to see she was following suit. He moved over to the blankets and spread out the picnic she'd packed as instructed. It was simple, but that's all they needed. With any luck at all, the wine would loosen her up a bit and they could move past the awkwardness that had suddenly bloomed between them.

"Will you join me?" He held out his hand, which she took, and together they sat.

"Malcolm, I'm not trying to be difficult. It's just—"

"Don't worry about it." He uncorked the wine and handed her an empty glass. "I'm not."

"It's just that I know you're trying to—"

"You don't know what I'm trying to do." He winked at her. No doubt she was getting annoyed that he kept cutting her off, but it was best to nip this train of conversation in the bud. "All I'm trying to do is enjoy your company. That's all." He poured some wine into her glass before he filled his own.

She looked as if she might protest again, but instead when Malcolm lifted his glass, she did the same and they clinked glasses with a smile. It didn't take long for them to fall into easy conversation as Kylie wanted all the details about the little cabin and how Malcolm could have kept it a secret from her for so long. As they spoke, they drank and Malcolm continued to fill her cup.

"If I didn't know better, I'd think you were trying to get me drunk." She smiled coyly and gave him as sexy little wink. All day, just being with her, he'd been in a semi-state of arousal, but that one simple action caused his cock to swell further. He had to maintain control. This had to be her idea.

"I don't know why you'd think that," he said as innocently as he could and picked up a cracker. "Tell me what's going on with you? How are things at the Paw? Samantha and Archer working you too hard?"

"Actually, I quit."

He almost choked on the cracker at the revelation. "You what?" How did he not know that little detail? At the very least, Archer should have told him. He made a note to have words with his friend as soon as he got a chance. "When?"

"Right after I saw you the other day. It was time."

"To quit your job?" He couldn't seem to understand what she was saying. Wasn't the whole reason they were broken up or on a break or whatever the hell she wanted to call it, was because she didn't want to quit her job and be dependent on him? "I don't get it. I thought your independence was important to you."

"It is."

"Then why would you quit?"

She put down her wine and got that serious look on her face. "My independence is important to me, not waitressing at a bar."

Something about her words made Malcolm remember the conversation he'd had with Archer. Had he, in all the time he'd been with her, ever asked her what she wanted to do? Did he know her dreams? Her goals? Once he had. Once he'd sat in this very cabin and listened to Kylie tell him all her hopes for the future. How had he forgotten that?

"Have you thought about nursing again?"

Her mouth fell open and she stared at him as if he'd just said the most amazing thing ever, which maybe he had because he, too, was surprised at himself.

"How did you…why did you…"

"I remembered you used to talk about wanting to be a nurse one day." He used his free hand to gesture around the small space. "You told me that right here. Don't you remember?"

"I do." She nodded. "I just didn't think you did."

Malcolm put his wine down and carefully picked up the leftover food, placing it behind him before he slid across the blanket to be closer to her. He took her hands in his and pulled them to his lips, where he placed a soft kiss on them. "I forgot for a while, but I remember now. I'm sorry."

For a moment, he thought she might cry, but instead she pulled her hands out of his grip and placed one on either side of his face. She rubbed her thumbs back and forth over his scruff before she pulled him down to her mouth.

Kylie's lips tasted sweet from the wine, a bit salty from the crackers, and perfectly delicious. It took a huge amount of willpower, but he let her take the lead on the kiss. It started soft and gentle, but soon a small groan escaped her lips and the scrap of control he had held on to snapped.

With a growl, he put one hand behind Kylie's head and pulled her tighter into him, increasing the intensity of the kiss. He needed to taste every inch of her mouth. And more. His other hand found her waist and gripped her through the soft fabric of her sweater. She responded with another moan, and Malcolm almost ripped her clothes off right then. He needed her with a ferocity he hadn't felt in…too long.

She broke the kiss and turned her head to the side; Malcolm used the opportunity to move his lips to her neck, kissing and nibbling with a hunger that was only barely contained.

"Malcolm, I—oh God that feels so…" Her words were lost and she trembled in his arms when his lips kissed her tender spot behind the ear.

He moved his attentions lower, to her collarbone, and

roughly pulled the sweater to the side. He needed there to be less clothing between him and his woman. His hands slid under the sweater, traveling over her flat stomach; he spread his fingers, wanting to feel as much of her as possible.

"Malcolm." She tried again. He knew he should let her say whatever she needed to say, but a bigger part of him, a part that was currently straining against his pants and throbbing with the need to be released, didn't want her to say a damned thing. Without wasting any more time, he yanked the sweater over her head and tossed it to the side to reveal a lacy black bra instead of the usual sports bra she would normally wear skiing. He looked at her, a question in his eyes to which she responded with a blush and a very slight shrug. "I thought maybe—"

"That our break would be over?" He took her face in his hands and kissed her possessively. She was his and dammit, he was going to do his best to show her that.

She pulled her mouth away again and growled low in her throat. The woman needed to stop doing that. "It's not over, Malcolm. This doesn't change anything."

He laid her back, hovered over her and stared directly into her eyes. "Why don't we wait before making any decisions?"

Chapter Nine

WITH MALCOLM STRADDLING HER BODY, his strong hands on her body, and that mouth that never failed to melt her on her neck, traveling lower once again, Kylie probably would have agreed to anything he said. And she'd meant what she said about this not changing anything. At least she thought she'd meant it.

But the way he kissed her, his heated mouth traveling all over her while his hands did the same, he was like a man possessed and who was she kidding. It was changing everything.

The rational part of her brain told her she needed to put a stop to what was happening. It wasn't right to give him mixed messages. If they had sex, that would only confuse the situation. They were supposed to be on a break and they couldn't be having much of a break if they were...oh God, it felt so good when he did that.

A low, sexy moan filled the small cabin and it took her a moment to realize that moan had come from her.

"Kylie, you are so gorgeous." Malcolm's voice was rough and thick with need. She opened her eyes to see him watching her. His lips turned up in to a killer smile when he saw her looking at him. Before she could respond to him, one hand cupped her breast and he used his thumb to roughly move over her nipple, peaking it to attention as the lace scraped against her sensitive bud. A spark of pleasure went straight into her core.

Did it really matter if they had sex? Her brain madly worked to justify the situation. It wasn't as if what they were doing was wrong. They practically lived together up until a few weeks ago, and technically…fuck technically. Kylie's hands flew up and under Malcolm's shirt, needing to feel his skin under her fingers. She was done trying to rationalize the situation. Hell, she was done thinking at all.

He grinned and gave her what she wanted. In a quick tug, he pulled his shirt off and over his head to expose his solid muscled chest. It was absolutely her favorite part of him. Well, one of her favorite parts. She trailed her fingers down his chest until she got to the waistband of his ski pants.

"Take them off." Her command was soft, but a command nonetheless.

His pupils dilated as passion flashed across his face. "You know I love it when you get bossy, but not today, babe." He jumped back, so he stood over her, bent at the waist, and it wasn't his pants he took off. Not at first anyway. His fingers made quick work of the button on her ski pants and he slid them down over her hips before he turned his attention to her leggings. "Damn, your legs look good in those." He stared at her appraisingly for a moment. "But they need to go, too." He tugged them down until she lay only in her lacy bra and matching panties, totally exposed in front of the fireplace. But she didn't feel exposed; she felt sexier and more desirable than she had in a long time. When was the last time Malcolm had taken the time to worship her body in this way?

Too long.

She used her eyes to gesture to the pants he still wore and with a devilish grin, he shed himself of those as well. As he stood over her, completely naked, the firelight danced off his skin. He was a force to be reckoned with. Her body shivered in anticipation, and judging by the look of him, she wasn't the only one excited.

"Get down here."

He didn't need to be asked twice. Malcolm once again straddled her body and she instantly wrapped her legs around him. She wanted him and she wanted him *now*.

"What did I say about being bossy?" He dropped a kiss on her neck, slowly worked his way down her body until she was forced to release her legs. He pushed the lace of her bra aside, forcing her breasts up and together before he sucked her nipple into his mouth and flicked it with his tongue. She let out an unexpected gasp and he growled appreciatively before he moved to give equal attention to the other breast.

Moving further south, Malcolm found the elastic waistband of her panties, but instead of pushing them down, he traced his fingers along the edge, down between her legs. Her entire body clenched with the anticipation of his touch, but he torturously walked his fingers over her thigh and away from her hot core.

"Malcolm," she complained. "Touch me." Her voice was breathy, and full of need, but he only chuckled and met her eyes again.

"I told you, you don't get to be bossy today."

The seriousness on his face, and the hot touch of his hands on her, only drove her crazier, but she knew pleading with him wouldn't make it happen any faster; it would only drag it out. And she was not in the mood to drag anything out. She wanted him now. And she knew one way to do it.

She smiled as seductively as she could. "Okay," she purred. "Whatever you say." She slid her hands between them and trailed them slowly down his abdomen until she reached the top of his thighs. She knew her man well enough to know exactly what would make him crumble.

Her man.

He was her man. Break or not, she had him exactly where she wanted him. One hand wrapped around to squeeze his ass while her other hand wrapped around his thick shaft. Instantly, Malcolm released a deep groan and she knew it wouldn't be long before she got exactly what she wanted.

She stroked up slowly, squeezing just enough as she moved.

"Kylie."

That was it, just one word. Her name. She paused and gave him a wicked little grin. She bit her bottom lip in the way she knew drove him crazy and continued to slide her hand up his length. He trembled beneath her touch. Time for the next step.

Kylie wiggled out from under him and despite their size difference, easily pushed him back so she was on top of him, and stared down into his lust clouded eyes.

"It's going to be like that, is it?"

She nodded.

The look in his eyes was intense and she knew in that moment if she wanted control of the situation, she'd have it. And not because Malcolm wanted her to take charge, because she knew from experience that he liked it best when he was in control of the situation. Just like life. He wanted to take care of her, make sure all her needs were met and for Malcolm, that meant being in control.

No, he would let her take control because he knew she needed it.

"Good."

She bent and kissed him with a ferocity she didn't even know she had. Not only had all the skiing built up the sexual tension between them, but being on top of him, the firelight flashing over his skin as the sunlight faded outside, had made her crazy. He returned the kiss, matching her intensity, and slid his hands all over her body while Kylie lifted her hips just enough before she lowered herself on top of him.

Her head fell back, and her hips stilled momentarily as she enjoyed the sensation of him inside her, filling her completely.

IT HAD BEEN TOO LONG. Way too long, and when she slid down on his shaft, Malcolm had to use all the self-control he possessed to keep from taking charge and driving into her the way he wanted to.

But she wanted to be in control, and he'd seen it in her eyes. She needed it. Things still weren't healed between them —he was smart enough to know that—and if she needed this, he was more than happy to give it to her.

She lifted her head up and looked at him before she bent to kiss him again. She tasted amazing. Sweet and spicy all at the same time. She tasted like his. He groaned into her mouth in an effort to let her know that his self-control could only last so long.

Kylie took the hint and moved her hips back and forth in a slow but steady rhythm. He knew he wouldn't last long, not with her watching him like that, with the sexiest little grin on her lips and her tongue running along her bottom lip.

"Woman, you are making me crazy."

"Good."

Kylie dropped down, so her breasts were pressed against him, and moved in a slow grind that she knew would drive him over the edge. He wrapped his hands around her round, firm ass and squeezed, encouraging her.

It didn't take long until he felt the familiar tightening of her body, and her breath came faster. Just listening to her, watching the changes on her face, the pleasure written all over it,

Malcolm felt the tug low in his groin that meant his own climax was imminent. He let her control the rhythm, using all his restraint to keep from quickening it the way he desperately wanted to.

But then it didn't matter as Kylie's eyes flew open, pinning him with her direct gaze as her entire body contracted into a long, hard climax. It put him totally over the edge as his own climax crashed into him. Malcolm kept his eyes open as well, letting her watch his climax the way he'd just watched hers. He couldn't hold back; he gripped her hips and pumped hard into her as he took his own release.

They stared at each other for a long time afterward, neither of them moving. He was afraid to look away, afraid it would break the connection they'd just forged, no matter how fragile.

He wasn't stupid, and he knew her well. Well enough to know that she was probably second-guessing what they'd just done. And he knew he couldn't let that happen. Before she could slide away, he wrapped his arms around her back and as gently as he could, he rolled them over so they lay side by side. He grabbed a blanket and pulled it up over their naked bodies and tossed another log in the fire before he laid back down, pulling her close so her head rested on his chest.

"Malcolm—"

"Ssh. Don't. Let's just enjoy this, okay?"

She stiffened in his arms and he knew he'd screwed up again. Dammit. He'd been doing everything right—he'd even let her take the lead with sex—and that was one area where he definitely liked to take the lead. What else could he do?

"Kylie, I wasn't trying to—"

"This doesn't fix anything."

What? Why the hell not? Not that he was stupid enough to think that sex would make their problems go away. But yeah, he'd hoped they would fix some of them. Or at least put them on the right track. He said as much.

"But it helps, right?"

She lifted her head so she could look at him and he did not like what he saw in her eyes. Indecision. Regret. Hell no. She was not going to regret having sex with him. No way.

He held up one finger. "Don't answer that. Not yet." He pushed himself up on one elbow, letting the blanket fall away. "Kylie, I love you. And I know you think you need a break to figure things out between us, but I'm trying here. And I need you to know that whatever it is that you need, I'll give it to you."

"That's the whole problem, Malcolm." She shook her head and turned away as she reached for her clothes.

"What's the problem? I don't understand what's going on." He knew he should stay calm. He knew he was totally blowing things, but he simply could not sit by and let her sabotage what they had and that's exactly what she was doing. "Kylie. Talk to me."

She spun around, her shirt in her hands. "I can't talk to you —that's the problem." She tugged her shirt over her head.

Malcolm jumped up and grabbed his ski pants and pulled them on. "What do you mean, that's the problem? We talk. We've been talking all afternoon."

"You don't understand."

"I'm trying! Tell me what to do and I'll do it, goddammit!"

"That's just it, Malcolm. You can't *give* me everything I need. You can't just wave your arm and make it all better."

"Why the hell not?"

He hadn't meant to raise his voice. The last thing he needed to do was push her away further than he already had. But things spiralled out of control too quickly for his liking. He needed to rein things back in, now. "I'm sorry. I didn't mean to yell." He reached out and pulled her in close.

Thankfully, she didn't pull away, so he wrapped his arms around her and nuzzled into her hair. "God, Kylie. I'm sorry."

He kissed her head tenderly and stroked her hair. "I'm trying to understand what's going on and I want to make this okay again. Hell, I *need* to make this okay again."

"I know." She nodded her head against his chest and he couldn't be certain, but he thought he heard her sniff. Damn. He didn't ever want to be the reason she cried. Before he could say anything else, she pulled back and wiped her eyes.

He knew he could protest further or continue pushing her and she might reveal something that could help him end the stupid break, but he also knew he had the potential to screw it up further. It was smarter to back off.

"Get dressed," he said with a nod. "I'll take you down the hill. I have a snowmobile parked out back. It's too dark to ski down."

For a second, she looked as if she might say something else, but he was glad when she didn't. They picked up their things, put out the fire, and Malcolm locked up and hid the key under the eaves, before he loaded their skis on the snowmobile. Kylie snuggled in tight behind him, wrapped her arms around his waist and rested her head on his back.

When they pulled up in front of the lodge, he helped her off the machine.

"Thank you for today, Malcolm. It was…it was perfect and I'm sorry it ended the way it did."

"You have nothing to be sorry for. I'm doing my best, Kylie. I'm listening and I know you said I can't fix it all, but I'm sure as hell going to try."

She opened her mouth to say something, but closed it again.

"You have to let me in, Kylie." He pulled her close and kissed her, slow and deep, because sometimes words weren't the best way to communicate.

Chapter Ten

TRUTH BE TOLD, when she'd quit her job, Kylie hadn't really thought it through. Heck, she hadn't thought past the moment. She definitely hadn't thought about how she was going to fill her days now that she wasn't working. For the first few, she'd been so busy working on the nursing school application and taking care of the errands that she'd let slide for the last few months that she hadn't given it any thought at all. But now that those items had been crossed off her list, Kylie was finding she had way too much time on her hands.

Time to think.

About Malcolm mostly.

And also their rendezvous at the secret cabin. That afternoon had played on an almost constant loop in her head. The man never failed to surprise her. How had she forgotten all about the place and yet he'd not only remembered, but also planned a romantic surprise? Maybe she'd been too hard on him. No, she *knew* she'd been too hard on him. He was trying. He was trying really hard. But he still kept missing the point.

That it had nothing to do with him. Not really anyway.

It was all making her head spin and hiding away in her tiny

house wasn't helping her any. She'd been hiding. From who or what, she wasn't sure, but she hadn't set foot outside since she'd returned from her rendezvous with Malcolm.

That had to change, and she knew exactly what she wanted to do. She picked up her phone and dialed the familiar number.

It only took two rings for Sam to pick up. "Hey, stranger. Don't tell me you want your job back." Sam's voice came across the line. "Because I'll give it to you, but I don't think—"

"No. Stop. I love you but I don't want my job back." Just speaking the words, she knew they were true. Kylie loved the Grizzly Paw, but it was time for a change. More than time.

"Well, that's good because I wasn't really going to give it to you." Sam laughed and Kylie couldn't help but laugh along with her. They'd been friends for so long, the familiar sound relaxed Kylie right to her core and she knew she'd made the right choice by calling her.

"I need a favor and it has nothing to do with a job."

"Anything," Sam said and Kylie knew she meant it.

"Are you doing anything today? I know it's last minute, but I need a girlfriend day. Is there anyway we can make—"

"Consider it done. I'll call some of the girls. What are we doing?"

There was no doubt in her mind what Kylie needed to do to relax and get her mind off everything. She told Sam her plan and after a few more minutes of discussion, she hung up, feeling better than she had in a long time.

The power of girlfriends was never to be underestimated.

"HEY BUDDY."

Malcolm looked up from his desk to see Seth in the door.

"You have time to take a break?"

He didn't. He had the latest numbers to look over and a report to craft for his investors, plus there was a message from Trent Harrison that had been sitting on the top of his to-do pile for most of the day. Despite working almost nonstop since his date with Kylie, he still wasn't caught up. Of course, there was the very real possibility that he was creating more work for himself in an effort to distract his mind from Kylie.

"Sure. Why not?" He pushed back from his desk. "What's up?"

Seth slapped his gloves into his bare hand and shook his head. "You definitely need a break from this office. When was the last time you got on the hill?"

Malcolm knew exactly when the last time he'd been on the hill was, and who he'd been with. And yes, he was well aware that as the owner of a ski hill, he probably should be making a point to get out on the hill more often, but he couldn't. Not without Kylie. "It doesn't matter."

"You're being a pussy. Snap out of it."

"Pardon me?" Malcolm rose from his chair and pulled his shoulders back in a way he knew was intimidating. It didn't matter that Seth was his number one man at the hill, or that without him he would have been lost over the last weeks. He was also his boss and he wouldn't stand for anyone talking to him like that. He clenched his fists and took as step toward his employee. "Do you want to say that again?"

"Stand down." Seth raised his hands and laughed. "I wasn't trying to offend you. I just needed to get you up and out of that chair. Seriously."

Malcolm took a step back and let his hands relax. He certainly didn't like it, but Seth had a point.

"What is going on with you?" Seth's tone turned serious, the laughter gone. "Your head hasn't been in the game since the opening, which is pretty much the exact opposite of how things should be. What the hell is going on?"

He opened his mouth to lash out at Seth. He knew damn well what was going on with him. Everybody in town knew what was going on. Hell, they'd all been there and witnessed the spontaneous combustion of his relationship in the middle of the friggin' New Year's Eve party. Malcolm swallowed his anger at the last moment and nodded. "I know."

"You know?"

"I know."

"Great. So do something about it."

Malcolm shook his head. Didn't he think he would have already done something about it if he could have? The problem was he had no clue what to do about it. He'd tried. He'd pulled out his big Valentine's surprise, made love to the woman he loved more than anything, and still, it wasn't good enough. What else was there to do?

Seth didn't wait for him to say anything. "Let's go." He smacked his gloves against the doorjamb and turned without waiting for an answer.

Malcolm stopped him before he left. "Go where?"

"I told you I had something to show you, and you need to get out of here. I may need to do some repairs up at the summit hut and I wanted you to tell me what you thought. Besides, the snow is fantastic. I think we both could do with a little stress relief in the form of fresh tracks off the summit."

Malcolm froze. "No."

"No to repairs on the hut?"

"No to fresh tracks." Malcolm grabbed his parka. "I'll take a snowmobile up and meet you there."

"Hell no, you won't. I need a buddy to ski with me."

Malcolm glared at his friend. "I don't pay you to ski."

"Sure you do." Seth laughed. "And you need to ski, too. That's why you got into this. It's important to remember that."

How was he going to explain that he didn't want to ski again unless it was with his woman? He pretty much couldn't explain it without looking exactly like the *pussy* Seth had accused him of. And he wasn't. He shook his head and just said it. "I won't ski without Kylie."

"What?" The admission obviously took Seth off guard and he laughed, but then he must have seen the look on his boss's face, because the laugh was quickly swallowed. "Seriously? I'm not trying to be a jerk, but that doesn't even make sense."

"I know."

"Besides. She's skiing without you."

"What?"

"Yup. Just saw her. Looks like they're headed up to the Platinum chair."

He shook his head and repeated himself. "What?" And then the second part of what he'd said hit him with a force that took him off guard. "Who's she with?" His mind immediately flew to thoughts of Kylie and Marcus shredding down the slopes the way he'd done with her only a few days ago. He hadn't seen Marcus for a few days either. Not since he'd watched him leave to move into one of the rooms at the lodge that Malcolm had set up for him. After all, he was his twin brother. It's not as if he was going to kick him out into the cold completely. Marcus had said he was going to try to win Kylie back, but dammit. He slammed his fist down on his desk. "Let's go."

"You don't want to know who she's with?"

"Hell no. Let's go skiing."

———

ALMOST IMMEDIATELY, the fresh air made Kylie feel better. Of course, her lighter mood probably had something to do with being surrounded by her girlfriends. Sam hadn't been fooling around when she said she'd make some calls. Beth Martin was still in town before heading out on her fiancé's next music tour, and she jumped at the chance to play hooky for the day and ski. As had Kari Fox, who was technically supposed to be working at the front desk of the Springs resort, but Sam pulled some strings with her husband Trent, who was part owner, and got her the day off as well. Cynthia promised to meet up with them later, when her part-time employee showed up for his shift at the store, and Bria Sheridan, who refused to learn how to ski or snowboard, was saving them seats in the lodge with promises of hot chocolate waiting for all of them when they had finished.

The four women rode up the Platinum quad chair, aptly named considering it took them to the best powder on the hill. As kids, they'd always rated the snow and the runs with Platinum being the highest rating they would bestow on their favorite runs. And Bronze was reserved for the bunny hill. When he reopened, Malcolm had renamed the chairs, using their nicknames. It was just one more example of his attention to detail and the way he honored their memories.

If he had such amazing attention to detail, why couldn't he figure out that she needed her own life separate from him? The thought popped into her head, drawing her away from the conversation the other women were having about Carmen and Dylan's baby and how cute he was. She'd resolved not to think about Malcolm or let him into her thoughts for the rest of the day, but clearly that resolution meant nothing.

"Earth to Kylie." Kari waved her hand in front of Kylie. "Are you still with us?"

She pasted a smile to her face. "Of course I am. I was just thinking about—"

"Malcolm." Samantha smiled innocently and Kylie glared at her.

"Maybe. But I'm trying not to. I really just want today to be about fun and forgetting about all the drama."

All three of her friends laughed. "Oh honey, you can't

make the drama just go away by ignoring it." Kari tried her best not to laugh. "It'll only get worse if you pretend it doesn't exist. Trust me on that."

It was true: if anyone knew about confronting your demons, it was Kari. She'd come to Cedar Springs with a fake name and an abusive ex-husband chasing her. It wasn't until she was honest with Rhys, who she'd also happened to have fallen in love with, that things got better for her. And now she was one of the happiest women Kylie knew.

She smiled warmly at her friend. "I know, Kari. You're right. But, I can't really confront what the problem is if I can't even explain it properly myself."

"Well, that's the problem then." Beth, who'd been quiet up until then, chipped in. "Let's figure out the problem so you can move on."

Kylie groaned. "Can we talk about something else?"

"No," her friends said in unison. They smiled sweetly and Kylie looked around her. Dangling from a chair ninety-five feet in the air, there really wasn't anywhere for her to escape to.

"Tell us what's going on," Samantha insisted. "What's really going on, not some bullshit answer. Malcolm's awesome and he loves you."

Kari nodded. "He'd do anything for you."

"That's the problem." Kylie blurted it out before she could stop herself. She put her hand over her mouth because there was no doubt her friends wouldn't understand.

And they didn't. "How exactly is that a problem?" Sam asked.

"I can't explain it."

"Try."

"I think I know what you're saying." Kylie turned to Beth, who looked at her with compassion. "I kind of have the same thing with Slade. He always wants to take care of everything so I don't have to worry about anything, and he has the means to do it, so he doesn't see what the problem is."

"And that's a problem?" Kari asked. "I don't get it. If your man wants to take care of you…"

"No." Kylie nodded. "I mean, yes. It is a problem. You're right, Beth. That's it. I worry that he thinks he's better than me, and he works so much that I barely see him and he has this amazing career and I don't have anything and I refuse to end up like my mother who just faded away with no identity at all because my father totally overshadowed her and even if I did have a career, would I be just like him and work all the time and forget about everyone in my life that I love and Malcolm only sees me as a waitress, not as an equal and I'm so much more than someone who serves his friends drinks at his own stupid party and why can't he see that I have dreams and goals too and I won't just be his little woman that he can take care of for the rest of his life." Kylie took a deep breath, exhausted from her outburst. Slowly, she turned to look at all three of her friends staring at her, their mouths open.

"Okay," Sam said slowly. "So I think we've just figured out what the problem is."

Before she, or anyone, could elaborate further, they reached the top of the hill, the safety bar was raised, and they all skied off the chair. Kylie didn't know whether she should be relieved or concerned. But when she skied over to the large wooden map that was their usual gathering place, she came to a snowy stop next to a familiar figure and she heard one of her friends mutter under her breath, "And…that might be another problem."

Chapter Eleven

HE KNEW before he even got on the chairlift that it was a bad idea. Despite Seth offering, more than once, to tell him who Kylie was with, Malcolm didn't want to know. Because he was pretty sure he already knew and he didn't want to know. Seth knew him well enough to know he was on edge, and he managed to fill the entire ride with chat about the hill and various things they needed to look at and take care of. Soon enough they crested the final rise and the top was in sight. Malcolm turned to lift the safety bar and his eyes froze on the sight he'd been hoping to avoid.

Or maybe not. Maybe he'd been hoping to see them together, to confront the situation head on. Either way, Kylie was standing with Marcus under the map.

"Hey, there's Marcus. I haven't seen him since—" Malcolm's glare cut off whatever Seth was going to say next.

As soon as Malcolm's skis touched the snow, he pushed off hard and skied directly over to them, stopping with a flurry of snow.

"Malcolm."

Kylie turned to him, a smile on her lips. Her cheeks were

pinked from the cold and she looked so damn beautiful, and in her element, that Malcolm's instinct was to reach out, pull her close and kiss her until her cheeks were pink for a different reason. "Nice to run into you," he said instead. "Marcus." He nodded an acknowledgement to his twin, but nothing more. "You two enjoying the hill today? It's a nice day for it."

Kylie's face twisted in confusion, the smile she'd worn a moment ago, gone. In contrast, Marcus grinned and it took all his self-control to not smack it off his face.

"We actually weren't—"

"It is a nice day." Marcus cut Kylie off. "We were just about to ski down the glades. Think you can keep up?"

Rage fueled through him, bubbling up into a competitive instinct that was completely primal.

Seth cleared his throat, bringing Malcolm back to the moment, and a hand smacked his arm, drawing his attention. "It's nice to see you, too, Malcolm," Samantha sassed him. Had she always been there? He looked around and saw the faces of Kari Fox and Beth Martin, too. Had they all...

Malcolm looked to Seth, who simply nodded and raised one eyebrow. He made a mental note to have a chat with him later about details that were not important versus details that were absolutely crucial to know going into a situation, and it definitely seemed that Kylie had been out skiing with the girls and not his brother. At least that's how it appeared, and in order to maintain what little self-control he had left, that was definitely the theory that he was going to run with.

"Hey, ladies," he said as casually as he could manage. "Enjoying your day, I hope." The women all gave him a combination of nods, head shakes, and grins in return, but he continued as if not every single person there didn't know that he was out-of-control jealous of his twin brother. "It's nice to see you all up on the hill."

"It's great to be back on the hill, Malcolm," Beth said. "I'm so glad it's all going so well." Her smile faded and she stumbled. "I mean, not everything obviously, but—"

In perfect public relations mode, Malcolm smiled and smoothed it over. "It's all going as well as can be expected with the launch of such a new project." He directed his gaze to Kylie, who watched him intently. "Every situation has a few bumpy spots, but it's nothing that can't be worked out with commitment and determination." She looked away but not before he thought he saw the flicker of a smile.

"Great," Marcus said, clearly growing bored with the conversation. "It's all great and everything's great. Now are we gonna lay tracks, or not?"

The women all whooped in agreement. All except Kylie, who looked back at him. "What about you, Malcolm?" she asked. "Do you have time to come for a run?" There was more to it than a simple question and Malcolm knew it.

Without hesitation, he replied, "Always." Whatever Seth had to show him could wait for later. He was pretty sure he could hear Marcus sigh in frustration, but he couldn't have cared less, especially when Kylie's smile told him he'd definitely made the right choice.

———

SHE HADN'T BEEN LOOKING to spend the day skiing with Malcolm again, but as unexpected as it was, it was nice, too. Especially with everyone all together. It was almost like the old days, and there was no pressure. It could have been weird having both brothers there, and it should have been weird. It might have been if it wasn't for her friends, who ran interference perfectly. Somehow they'd managed to split up to ride up the chair, which meant Kylie was with first Beth, and then Kari, while the other ladies rode up with the Stone brothers and Seth. She made a mental note to thank her friends later.

She was having too much fun racing everyone down the hill and laying fresh tracks on the powder to worry about anything more pressing than which run to take next. And that definitely included any major relationship decisions. Instead, she focused on the heat in her muscles as she leaned in to every turn, concentrated on cutting a line down the hill. She put all her focus into skiing, which meant there was no room for anything else. It also meant she was making record times during the runs.

Despite her fast times, she was tiring, and Malcolm was still beating her down the hill. As was Marcus. But just barely. As she crested the last ridge, she saw both brothers standing together at the bottom of the hill. The sight threw her off. It was like a blast from the past to see them both there together like that. As she skied closer, her eyes went to only one man.

Malcolm.

It had always been Malcolm. It had just taken her a few years to figure that out, and even with Marcus standing right there next to him, there was no contest.

She came to a stop in a shower of snow that covered both of them.

"Nicely done, Wilson." Marcus laughed. "You still have some skills."

"Some?"

"She's got all kinds of skills." The comment came from Malcolm. She stared at him, and laughed.

"It's true. I do."

Moments later, the rest of the group showed up.

"Damn, you guys are too fast." Samantha folded over in an effort to catch her breath. "I clearly need to get out here more."

Kari pulled her goggles up onto her helmet. "I don't know about the rest of you, but I think it's après-ski time."

"Absolutely." Beth was quick to chime in. "I'm more than

ready for a drink. Besides, Bria's holding seats for us. We should get in there."

The women glanced between Kylie and the men, but before an invitation could be issued, Seth, who'd taken a detour, showed up.

"I should probably do some actual work today," Malcolm said with a glance toward Seth, who agreed. "And I'm sure Marcus probably has some training or something to do, don't you, Marcus?"

The showdown between the brothers wasn't subtle, and the last thing Kylie wanted was a confrontation of any kind, but she wasn't getting involved. The days of getting between the brothers was over. They needed to sort out whatever was going on between them, even if it had to do with her. Especially if it had to do with her.

"Okay then," she said quickly. "It was fun, guys, thanks."

She was about to ski her way over to the lodge when Malcolm said, "We'll have to do it again, soon."

He'd said it casually but Kylie knew the comment was loaded with all kinds of meaning. Her smile was genuine when she looked him in the eyes. "Absolutely."

The girls all made their way to the lodge, took off their skis, and headed inside to warm up. Kylie was about to follow suit, when a voice stopped her. She turned, her skis still in one hand.

"Do you have a second?" Marcus stood, his arm around his snowboard.

Talking to Marcus was probably not a good idea, especially considering what happened the last time they'd had a *conversation*. She glanced around to look for backup, but the girls had already gone inside.

It wasn't a big deal anyway. She sighed. "What's up?"

"Don't sound so excited."

She tilted her head and gave him a look. "The girls are waiting. What's up, Marcus?"

For a moment, she thought she saw a dip in his normally unflappable confidence, but then he grinned and leaned toward her. "We had fun today."

"We did."

"We used to have fun like that all the time and then—"

"That was a long time ago." She knew where he was going with such a line of conversation and she wanted none of it. "Marcus…" She saw his face change and in that moment, Kylie knew he finally understood. "I need you to understand—"

"I know." His smile held a measure of regret. "It's Malcolm."

She nodded.

"It's always been Malcolm, hasn't it?"

She was going to tell him no, that there'd definitely been a time when it was him that she thought she was in love with. Instead, Kylie smiled and nodded. "Always."

"I know." She'd never seen Marcus look so pensive, so… regretful, and she hated that she might be hurting his feelings, but she couldn't focus on that. It wouldn't be fair to anyone. He shrugged and his handsome smile was back. "I blew it; I get that." He reached out and touched her cheek gently before he pulled away.

"He loves you, Kylie. I think he might love you even more than you think he does. Whatever's going on, just remember that, okay?"

In all the years she'd known the Stone brothers, Kylie had never heard Marcus put his twin brother first. Maybe he was growing up.

She smiled kindly. There might have been once, but there were no longer any hard feelings between them. "I'll see you around, Marcus." She gestured to the lodge, where her friends were waiting. "I should get going."

"Of course."

He grabbed his board and turned to leave. She watched him for a minute before she called after him. "Be happy, Marcus."

He turned and gave her a wink and blew her a kiss. "Advice to live by, Kylie."

"IT'S NOTHING."

Malcolm turned and glared at Seth, who'd seen him watching the exchange between Kylie and Marcus. It wasn't nothing. His brother had touched her. Sure, they hadn't kissed again but...he growled, his possessive nature consuming him.

"Seriously," Seth said again as they moved forward in the lift line. "It's nothing. She's allowed to talk to him."

With an urge to punch his friend, Malcolm turned back to the scene he couldn't help but watch. Marcus blew her a kiss and she'd smiled. But he'd left. There'd been no actual kiss, not that he really thought she'd kiss him. Not after...he shook his head in an effort to clear it.

"We're holding up the line." Seth tugged on his jacket. "Our turn."

They skied forward and got on the chair, where they sat in silence for half the ride. He hated how jealous he got where his brother was concerned, but what other response was there? With their history and Kylie breaking things off...nothing made sense.

"You know it's not Marcus she wants to be with, right?"

Malcolm was so caught up in his own head, it took him a second to realize Seth was talking to him. "What did you say?"

"It doesn't take a genius to see that she's in love with you."

His friend didn't know what he was talking about and as much as he wanted to believe what he said, it couldn't be true. If Kylie was in love with him, they would be together right now instead of doing this…whatever it was they were doing.

"It's true." Seth kept talking. "Cynthia told me she's just going through some stuff but it has nothing to do with you."

"First of all, if it has nothing to do with me, I'd be there helping her go through whatever *stuff* she needs to go through. That's what boyfriends do," Malcolm said, and then looking for a way to change the subject, he added, "And what do you mean by, *Cynthia says?*" Malcolm raised his eyebrow at his friend. "Since when do you chat with Cynthia?"

He shrugged and looked away. "We've known each other for years."

"Maybe…"

"What?" Seth turned back and Malcolm laughed. There was clearly something more than his buddy was telling him. "We talk sometimes," Seth offered.

"Like when?"

"What's with the interrogation? We were talking about you and Kylie."

"No. We're talking about you and Cynthia."

"There is no me and Cynthia."

"But you want there to be?"

It probably wasn't fair to pick on Seth, but Malcolm couldn't help it and to his surprise, he was actually having a little bit of fun.

"She's hot," Seth said.

Malcolm glanced forward; they were getting close to the top of the lift. "Why do I get the feeling that that's definitely not it? Have you slept with her?"

Seth didn't answer right away the way Malcolm expected. He knew his buddy well, and he'd never been one of those guys who liked to brag about conquests. He'd also been one of those guys who didn't settle down or take any type of relationship with a woman seriously. If Cynthia was getting involved with him, she might not like the way it ended up. Not that it was his responsibility. But maybe he should tell Kylie...

"None of your business." The look in Seth's eyes warned Malcolm off pushing it any further, but he didn't totally dismiss the idea of talking to Kylie about it, if things ever settled down with them.

"Come on." Seth pulled his goggles down over his eyes. "Let's go check the ski patrol cabin. I think we'll need some sort of insulation on the windows. The space heater isn't doing the job."

Malcolm let him change the subject and together they skied off the chair and went to take care of business. He spent his afternoon immersed in the daily upkeep issues of the ski hill, but no matter how busy he tried to be, the only thing he could think of was Kylie.

HER DAY with the girls had been exactly what Kylie'd needed. Even when the guys joined them, it was still fun, maybe more so. Immediately after her talk with Marcus, it was like a weight of worry and stress had been lifted and she could finally breathe and focus on what was important. From the moment he'd walked into the New Year's party, he'd only added to her confusion about everything. Now that she'd sorted that out in her head, she finally felt as if she could figure out everything else and get back to being happy.

Of course, after she'd finally gone into the lodge to have a drink with the girls, they'd been chomping at the bit to hear all the gory details of what Marcus had said and whether he was the reason she'd decided on the break with Malcolm. All their questions had made her head spin, but she knew they were only trying to be good friends, so she told them the truth.

"There's nothing between me and Marcus."

Sam nodded, but Beth looked as if she was going to disagree. Kylie continued before she could say anything. "There never really was anything between us. Nothing real anyway. Not like…"

"Malcolm?" Kari smiled innocently and sipped at her hot chocolate.

She was right, though. Whatever she might have once had with Marcus, it was nothing compared to the way things were with Malcolm.

Or had been.

She pushed the thought away and took the mug Bria handed her with a nod of thanks.

"I know I'm new," Bria said, "but is it okay if I say something?"

"Of course." They all nodded. As far as the girls were concerned, once you were in, you were in.

Bria flipped her hair back. "I know what it feels like to be unsure of something. I also know that pushing away the ones who care about you the most while you're trying to sort things out is almost always going to be a decision you'll regret."

Her words hit Kylie in the chest. Bria was right. Part of Kylie had regretted the way she'd pushed Malcolm away almost immediately after she'd done it. But there was another part that knew she'd made the right choice, taking the break when she did. She never would have had the space or courage to apply for nursing school if she hadn't. She would have kept on doing what she was doing, getting pushed aside as Malcolm took care of business, forgetting her own dreams. She would have turned into her mother.

"I know what you're saying." Kylie straightened her shoulders. "But don't you think it's possible to get so wrapped up in a relationship that you forget who you really are and who you want to be?"

The women were all quiet; likely they each pondered their own situation. They were all madly in love with the men who were perfect for them and for the most part, all of Kylie's friends knew what they wanted to do with their life and they'd been doing it.

Kari cleared her throat. "I agree with you, Kylie."

All heads turned to Kari, who shrugged sweetly. "Don't forget," she said. "I had a whole life before Rhys. A life I hated." She looked over to Kylie and added quickly, "I'm not saying you hate your life." Kylie shook her head and smiled before Kari would continue. "But I get what it's like to feel trapped."

"Your situation was a bit different." It was Sam who interjected. They all remembered what Kari had been through, running from her abusive ex. Malcolm could definitely not be compared to him, but Kari had a point.

"And now things are different for you?" Kylie asked her. "I mean, are you happy with what you're doing now?"

"For now." She nodded. "I'm not going to work at the front desk of the Springs forever. But for right now, I'm just enjoying my life. The time will come for me to figure out the future, but when I do, I'll do it with Rhys." She looked pointedly at Kylie.

"The way I should be doing it with Malcolm?"

Her friend smiled sweetly. "You said it. Not me."

Kylie couldn't think of a reply to that comment, and fortunately for her, she didn't have to. The arrival of Carmen with little Hunter distracted everyone from her relationship problems. They all fussed over Hunter while Carmen told them all about the Mommy and Me music class she was taking with *Ms. Holly* in the village.

Kylie let herself get lost in the flurry of conversation, but Kari's words replayed in her mind. Maybe she should have discussed everything with Malcolm. Sure, sometimes it seemed as if the only thing he was worried about was the ski hill, but that was to be expected, wasn't it? And hadn't he surprised her with the hut? Memories of their lovemaking in front of the fire flooded her senses, but it was something he'd said that stuck with her. At the time, she hadn't pursued it, because something else had come up and she'd been a little taken off guard by the whole situation. But she'd certainly remembered it.

Malcolm had asked her about nursing. It was something she'd said in passing all those years ago, and never brought up again, but somehow he'd remembered. Was it the ski hut that had sparked his memory? Did it matter?

The conversations going on around her grew muted as Kylie ran through the past few weeks in her head. Everything was so screwed up, and she knew it was her fault. All this time she'd been so worried about becoming her mother or her father that she'd forgotten who she was, and if she wasn't careful, it wasn't only herself she'd lose—it was Malcolm, too.

Chapter Twelve

"WHAT HAPPENED TO YOU YESTERDAY?"

Kylie leaned up against the counter and watched Cynthia shelve some chocolate bars. She hadn't made it up for après-ski drinks the day before, and when Kylie had tried to call her, she hadn't answered. It was unusual, and with the sketchy way Cynthia wouldn't meet her eye, Kylie knew something was up.

"I had to work," she answered without turning around. "Colton was sick or something, so he couldn't come in and I can't just leave the shop to go for drinks, Kylie. You know that."

"I do know that." She shifted around, so she'd be facing Cynthia when she looked up. "I also know you weren't home when I tried calling you later. Were you still here?"

"Totally. I had some inventory come in and had to get to it right away."

"Bullshit."

Cynthia's head shot up and she stared at Kylie, who had her arms crossed over her chest, feeling particularly smug.

"I called you here, too."

Cynthia turned an interesting shade of red; an unfortunate side effect of being a redhead was the giveaway blush. A fact Kylie had used to her advantage for years.

"What's going on? Spill."

Her friend finished putting away the chocolate bars and reluctantly turned and leaned against the opposite counter. "I didn't want to tell you," she said. "You have enough going on and you've been so preoccupied with everything that you haven't really been very available."

That stung. "What? I'm always available." She knew it was a lie. She had definitely not been available lately. "Okay, I know. I know." She grabbed a bag of M&M's and tore it open. "I'm sorry. I know I've been a total mess lately and a terrible friend. Tell me, please. I promise, I'll listen." She passed the bag over to Cynthia, who only raised her eyebrow. "I'll pay for it." Cynthia smiled and took some candy.

"Honestly, there isn't much to tell." She popped the M&M's in her mouth and walked around the other side of the counter.

"What?" Kylie was right on her tail. "That's it? There's nothing much to tell? You got me all worked up and made me feel bad for that?"

Cynthia laughed and after a moment, Kylie joined in. "Seriously," she said after a moment. "What's going on, Cyn? Is everything okay with you?"

She grabbed the bag from Kylie's hand. "Nothing a bit of chocolate can't fix."

Kylie knew her friend well enough to know when she didn't want to talk. She also knew that Cynthia would talk about whatever it was when she was ready. Pushing her would only shut her down. She snatched the bag back and tossed some candy into her hand. "Chocolate fixes everything."

"Especially man problems."

Kylie gave her a pointed look.

"I meant your man problems," Cynthia said. "Are they fixed yet?"

She threw the now empty candy bag back at her friend. "Do you have any more chocolate?"

"That good, huh?"

It's not that it was bad. It was just that it wasn't that good either. It was somewhere in that in-between place where she hadn't dealt with anything at all. She'd spent the whole night tossing and turning, thinking about what she really wanted to do. And the more she thought about it, the thought of losing Malcolm terrified her almost as much as spending her whole life not realizing her dreams or finding her purpose. She didn't want to continue being only *Malcolm's girlfriend*; she needed more. That being said, she also needed Malcolm. Now she just needed to figure out how she could have it all and the first step was talking to Malcolm.

Kylie shook her head. "I need to talk to Malcolm. I think it's finally time I told him what's been going on in my head."

"That would be a good first step." Cynthia winked. "And it's about time, too."

"I know. And I know it sounds stupid, but I think I really needed this time to be sure about everything. Do you know I applied for nursing school?" Saying the words aloud for the first time was freeing, and also terrifying. "I probably won't get in," she continued. "But I had to do it. I need to do something. It's time."

Cynthia looked as though she were going to cry. "I'm so proud of you."

The serious look on her friend's face made Kylie laugh.

"No," Cynthia said, her tone serious enough to dry up Kylie's laughter. "I mean it. I am. And you will totally get in."

"I don't think I will." Kylie raised her hand to stop the

protest she knew would come. "And I'm not trying to be self-deprecating. I'm serious. I'm an older applicant and they probably have a lot more qualified people applying. Besides, it's probably a good thing if I don't get in."

"Why?"

"Because I love Malcolm. I know that now more than ever, and I can't be with him if I have to move away to go to school."

"That's the dumbest thing I've ever heard."

She shrugged and grabbed her coat. "Maybe. But I guess it's all a moot point if I don't go find him and tell him I love him, isn't it?"

That made Cynthia smile and she pulled Kylie into a hug. "Go do that. Everything else will fall into place."

As Kylie left the store and made her way up the icy mountain road to the hill, Cynthia's words kept repeating in her head. She hoped her friend was right but she had a bad feeling that things weren't going to be as easy as she thought.

IT HAD BEEN TOO long since Malcolm had been up to the Springs resort. Not that he'd had much reason to visit the exclusive resort in the last few months, but just wandering down the main corridor, with its wall of glass facing the mountains beyond, made him question why he hadn't found a reason. The resort was beautiful. Every detail had been considered and the result was a building that was completely in sync with the rugged beauty that surrounded it. The glass wall made it feel as if you were right outside and could simply reach out and touch the mountains. When Trent and Dylan Harrison designed the building, they made sure the healing water for which the resort was named for had been incorporated throughout as well, which meant there were no shortage of fountains and pools everywhere Malcolm looked. The burbling sounds filled the air, and created a sense of calm.

It truly was a beautiful place and it was easy to see how it could be a romantic destination, too. With the right person. With Kylie.

Maybe she'd allow him to take her for a date and he could have Jax Carver, the head chef, prepare a special meal for them, and afterwards, he'd take her to one of the private pools where they'd let the therapeutic water work its magic on them. Malcolm was so lost in the fantasy, he'd completely forgotten why he was at the Springs in the first place, until Trent slapped him on the back.

"Sorry I'm running late, buddy."

Malcolm recovered quickly and took Trent's hand. "No problem. I was just enjoying the view. It's pretty incredible. I know I spend my days actually on the mountain, but there's something about the way you've done this here, it's…"

"I know. Pretty amazing. I have to give Dylan most of the design credit, though." He smiled and was immediately down to business. "Are you hungry? Jax said something about bison burgers today and sometimes I'm in the mood for a good burger."

"Absolutely. I can always eat and when Jax is cooking… hell, sounds perfect."

It wasn't until they were seated in the Stillwater restaurant that the men got down to business. "I'm glad you finally called me back, Malcolm. I know you've had a lot going on lately."

"But we're not here to talk about my personal life." There was no doubt that Trent knew all about his issues with Kylie, especially considering his new wife Samantha had spent the day skiing with her. She'd also no doubt witnessed the exchange between Kylie and Marcus and probably knew more about the situation than he did. Still, that was the last thing he wanted to talk about at the moment.

"No, we're not." Trent grinned and raised his beer. "Women." He shook his head and Malcolm laughed.

"Women." Malcolm met him in an easy toast and they drank to their mutual confusion over the opposite sex.

"Okay, what I really wanted to talk to you about was something that I think will benefit both of us a great deal."

"I like those kinds of talks."

"I thought you might." Trent produced a folder. "This is what I'm thinking. We're both businessmen, and we both have unique experiences to offer guests."

Malcolm nodded and Trent slid a sheet of paper across the table for him to examine.

"But you lack rooms for your guests." Malcolm looked up, fairly sure where Trent was going. "And I lack a ski hill."

They chuckled. "That's a fact."

"So what do you think?" Trent gestured to the sheet and Malcolm scanned it quickly, liking what he saw.

Trent proposed a variety of ski and spa packages that would benefit both of them. "How do you feel about a few joint marketing efforts?" Trent asked. "I think it could really work. We'd be able to offer a one-stop destination in Cedar Springs."

Malcolm nodded. The more he looked at what Trent had put together, the more he liked what he saw. It would definitely benefit both of them and a brand new ski hill could be a precarious investment; he was more than happy to partner up for some guaranteed guests.

"This is fantastic, Trent. Really. I think this could work out really well. Thanks for thinking of me."

"Hey, don't kid yourself," Trent said with a laugh. "This is a mutually beneficial situation. I'm looking forward to working with you, buddy." He raised his glass again and this time when they toasted, it was to continued success for both of them.

As much as Malcolm wanted Stone Summit to be successful, there was something, or rather, someone missing from the picture. He needed to talk to Kylie. This break thing was getting ridiculous, and it was time they sat down and hashed it all out. But first he needed nourishment and when Jax came out of the kitchen and personally delivered the burgers, Malcolm tucked into his meal, enjoying every bite. After a bit more chatting, Malcolm was itchy to get going and track down Kylie, so he made his excuses and was almost out the front door when he saw a familiar face chatting up the girl at the concierge desk.

Marcus.

Of course he would run into him here; Trent and Dylan had been nice enough to give him a place to stay when Malcolm kicked him out. Malcolm hadn't considered that when he'd decided to hold their meeting at the Springs.

Maybe it was his state of mind, or maybe it was just that he was fed up with his brother and the way he treated women, but watching Marcus flirt so shamelessly made him clench his fists. Only a few days ago, his brother had declared his intentions to go after Kylie—not that he had a chance in hell with Malcolm's woman, but still. Did he not have any shame at all? The familiar anger that seemed to show up whenever Marcus was around filled him. Malcolm changed course and stalked over to his brother.

"So a few days ago you were making the moves on *my* woman." He made sure to emphasize that she was his. "Hell, Marcus, you even kissed her in a move that only reeked of desperation. And now you're hitting on this poor girl." He looked at the woman, who did not seem to be under any duress caused by Marcus's attention. In fact, she looked amused. "Can we talk somewhere?" he asked Marcus.

They walked a few feet away. It was Marcus who spoke first. "I don't want to fight with you, Malcolm." He held up his hands in defense. "We've gotta call a truce. This has to stop."

"What needs to stop is the way you treat Kylie." He all but growled the last word.

"Pardon?"

"She's mine."

"I know."

"You need to back off once and—what?"

"I said, I know. She's yours," Marcus said. "I know that. I've always known that. Hell, even when she was with me, she was yours, Malcolm. I know that."

His head spun as he tried to keep up with what his brother said.

"Why do you think I went out with her all those years ago?" Marcus didn't wait for a reply, which was good because Malcolm was still trying to process what he'd heard. "I knew you liked her, and I was pretty sure had I given it a chance, she would have been into you."

"So you—"

"Asked her out before that could happen."

Malcolm ran a hand through his hair and stared at his twin. "Why?"

"You had everything, Malcolm. Popular, smart...hell, you were going to do something with your life. You had it all. I just wanted something you couldn't have."

"What? You're telling me that you dated Kylie because you were jealous and wanted to keep her from me?" He balled his hands into fists again. His fingers twitched to make contact with his brother's nose.

Marcus nodded, but to his credit he didn't look smug or even satisfied in any way about what he'd done. "I know it was stupid, but we were kids and I was jealous. You were the super-star twin and I was—"

"The professional snowboarder." It was crazy how they both had such different perceptions of how things really were. "You were a star from the moment you strapped that board to your feet, and when we moved to Cedar Springs, it was you all the girls wanted. You were the one with the future." He shook his head. "This is crazy."

"Look, it was stupid. I'm sorry, Malcolm."

He wanted to believe him. He did. But there was something else Malcolm needed to know before he accepted any apologies. "What about the kiss?"

"She kissed me, man."

Malcolm almost hit him right then and there, and the raw anger must have shown on his face because Marcus took a quick step back. "It didn't mean anything, Malcolm. Shit, relax, okay?"

He didn't relax his fists, but Malcolm nodded so Marcus would continue. "I was in the right place at the wrong time, that's it. I know that meant nothing. Not to me, and not to her. I know that because she told me so. And the other day at your house, all that talk about winning her back?" Malcolm nodded. He remembered. "I was jealous, man. Again, you have everything. For God's sake, you own the ski hill. You have these great friends, this incredible life, and a woman who loves you."

Malcolm's chest constricted at that. Did she still love him?

"I just wanted to piss you off," Marcus continued. "Because even if I wanted Kylie, there is no way I could have her. She loves you, Malc. She loves you more than even she knows."

Malcolm's shoulders sagged; his hands uncurled at his sides. His brother's declaration had taken him off guard and even though not one punch was thrown, he felt as though he'd been in a brawl. "I hope that's true," was all he could manage to say.

Marcus stepped forward and put his hand on his shoulder.

The brotherly touch felt good and despite everything between them, it felt right. "It's true, Malc. I know it."

He looked up into his brother's identical face and nodded. "I'm sorry, Marc."

"Yup. I know. Me too, man." Without warning, Marcus landed a punch on Malcolm's arm, which he returned. They both laughed, and just like that, Malcolm had his twin brother back. And it felt damn good.

Chapter Thirteen

WHEN KYLIE COULDN'T FIND Malcolm at the ski hill, she'd decided to get in a few runs while she waited for him. He'd be back in the office; he always was. Besides, the snow was too good to pass up and now that she'd rediscovered her passion for skiing, it was getting harder and harder to watch without getting on the hill herself. She'd left her equipment in a locker in the lodge, and still had her ski clothes in the car, so in less than ten minutes she was ready to go. Moments before she pushed her way over to get in the lift line, her cell phone vibrated in her pocket. Thinking it had to be Malcolm, she pulled it out and answered it before she looked at the caller ID.

"Ms. Wilson?" A voice that was definitely not Malcolm's came over the line.

"Yes?"

"This is Brenda Norton from the admissions office at Western Nursing Academy. I'm sorry—we don't usually make personal calls. I hope I didn't catch you at a bad time."

Kylie's heart raced in her chest. Had they seriously called her personally to let her know that her application was denied? Maybe she'd missed something on the form. "It's fine."

"Like I said, we don't usually make personal calls but we received your application this morning and although we'd already finalized the admissions for the next semester, there's an opportunity we feel you'd be perfectly suited for, if you're interested?"

She had no idea what possible situation it could be, but there was no doubt about it; she was interested. "Of course."

The woman, Brenda Norton, went on to explain the opportunity for Kylie to enter an express nursing program that would fast-track her through her classes. Based on her age and transcripts, they liked to accept more mature students because the program was so much more intense than the regular program, and they'd just had a cancellation, so if Kylie was interested, they would enroll her to start in the upcoming session.

Of course she was interested.

Kylie hung up the phone with a surge of emotions rolling through her. Excited? Definitely. Terrified? For sure. Unsure? A little bit. Okay, more than a little bit. A lot. Becoming a nurse was her childhood dream—besides going to the Olympics, of course. She'd totally shelved it when she was a teenager, because it had been way more fun to ski and party. And then it finally just got easier to put her dream on the shelf than to deal with the reality of it. But now the reality stared her in the face and it was even scarier than she'd ever imagined.

And exciting. It was really exciting, too.

She tucked her phone away and pushed herself into the chairlift line. She needed to think and burn off some of the energy she was feeling and the best way to do that was to cut through some fresh powder. It would give her time to process the one little detail that was stopping her from being thrilled with the whole idea of going to school.

After Brenda Norton explained the unique opportunity,

she'd also told Kylie that the start date was for the spring semester. Six weeks away.

Six weeks.

She rode the chair up to the top of the mountain, but the ride did nothing to help clear her mind. She needed to talk to Malcolm, but was it fair to him to tell him that she loved him and wanted to be with him when she'd be turning around and leaving? The program ran for twenty-four months, with only a few breaks in between. Then she'd have to do a practicum, and even if she tried, she might not get one in Cedar Springs. In theory, she could be away for a few years. That wasn't fair to Malcolm.

By the time she skied off the chair and headed for the glades, she was no closer to figuring things out. If anything, she was more confused. Time to stop thinking and just let her body take over. She pushed hard and picked a line through the trees right next to the out-of-bounds line. She cut through the snow hard, enjoying the fact that she was all alone on the hill. Not many people came so far over in the glades; it took an experienced skier, who knew what they were doing, to handle the snow so far back.

She cleared the first thicket of trees and came to a stop on the edge of the next section. So deep in the trees, the way she was, there was no view to speak of, and the thick evergreens muted the sunlight and muffled any sound. Not that there was a lot of noise so far back in the trees.

"Hey!"

The voice took her off guard and she spun to look for the source.

"Let's go over here."

The voice was close, but not too close, and it certainly wasn't addressing Kylie. She saw a flash of movement slightly farther down the hill: a bright pink jacket, followed by a lime green one. Very few people ever ventured off the groomed runs, and they sounded like kids. Curious, Kylie made her way toward them. As she drew close, she could see that she recognized the girl in the lime green jacket: Jules, Beth's daughter who'd delivered the backpack to her. The girl in the pink must be a friend. Either way, they stood way too close to the out-of-bounds area. In fact, their skis were hanging off the edge that would take them directly into the area that was neither patrolled by ski patrol nor maintained by Stone Summit.

Not good.

"Jules!" She yelled, trying to get their attention, but she was too far away and the girls had obviously already made up their mind because they pushed off with their poles and disappeared beneath the ridge.

"Crap." Kylie didn't even think about what she was doing, just pushed herself into action and skied after them. If they were going out of bounds, there was no telling what could happen.

SHE WASN'T FAR behind them, but the girls must have been better skiers than she gave them credit for because Kylie had trouble catching up with them. She pushed a little harder, scanning the area in front of her to look for a flash of color between the trees or anything that would help her find the girls. If everything went well, they'd be able to ski right out and back onto the groomed run.

If everything went well.

If it didn't, Kylie wanted to be there.

She stopped to catch her breath and look around. The snow was deeper back here, and Kylie wasn't familiar with the terrain. A flash of pink in the trees to her left caught her attention. The girls. She must have somehow gone past them.

Jules, in her green jacket, came into her line of sight and then she was gone in a puff of snow. "Jules!"

Kylie skied over to where she'd seen her. The bright green of her jacket was half covered by the powder. Kylie dropped to her knees. "Jules. Jules, are you okay?" She dug away the snow and grabbed Jules by the shoulder to turn her over. Her eyes were open. Thank God, she was awake.

"Kylie?"

"Does it hurt anywhere?"

"My knee." Tears sprang to her eyes. "Oh my God, my knee. Kylie, it hurts."

"I know. I know. It's okay." Kylie glanced around. "Your friend, what's her name?"

"Tori."

Kylie took off her gloves and wiped the tears from Jules's face. "It's going to be okay, I promise. Let's get the ski off, okay?"

Jules nodded and bit her lip, so Kylie quickly popped her own skis off and placed them upright in the snow in an X. "Tori?" Kylie yelled and scanned the hill for the pink jacket. "Tori?"

Seconds later, the pink jacket came into view. The girl, obviously struggling with the challenging terrain, step-skied her way toward them. "Oh my goodness, Jules. What happened? Are you okay?"

"She's fine," Kylie said. "I assume you're Tori?" She had to bite her tongue from giving the girls trouble about skiing in an out-of-boundaries zone. There'd be time for that later. For the moment, she needed to look at Jules's ski. "Help me get her ski off."

To her credit, Tori moved quickly and without protest. They got Jules's ski off and managed to dig out the snow around her and make a sort of chair. Remembering her basic first aid training, she knew she needed to get it elevated and there was definitely no skiing on it.

"What are we going to do, Kylie? I can't stay here and the

sun's going to go down and…it hurts. It really hurts." Tears sprang to her eyes, but the girl fought hard to maintain some semblance of teenage bravado. She swallowed hard and struggled to ski. "I can stand."

"No, you can't." Kylie held her down. "I'll call for help." She pulled her cell phone out of her pocket and groaned when she saw there was no service. Of course there wasn't. She looked around again and tried to figure out exactly where they were and when they'd left the boundary. If she wasn't mistaken, she wasn't too far from the little cabin, but she couldn't get Jules there. Not on her own and not with only another thirteen-year-old girl to help. She looked at Tori. She didn't know Jules's best friend, but she'd heard Beth talk about her; Beth seemed to think she was fairly responsible and besides that, she didn't have any other choices. "Tori, you're going to have to go for help."

Tori opened her mouth to object, but Kylie cut her off. "We don't have another choice. You have to be strong and do this, okay?"

The girl nodded.

"You're a strong skier; you'll be fine. I just need you to stay to your right. Keep pushing to the right and soon you'll be back out on the groomed run." Kylie wasn't entirely sure that was true, but she needed to tell Tori something and despite the fact that she could have been sending the girl into a scenario where she would get lost all alone, Kylie believed enough in her sense of direction that it would be okay. It had to be.

"You're sure?"

"I am." Kylie nodded. "That's how you were going to go, wasn't it?"

"I think so."

Kylie bit back her comments on the irresponsibility of skiing out of bounds with no real plan to get back. She tried to remember she was a teenager once and she'd probably done irresponsible things. Yes, she'd definitely done irresponsible things.

"You'll be fine. I know it." She did her best to keep her voice optimistic. "Just move as fast as you can and be safe. It's not too much farther."

Kylie watched her go. She skied well, as if her life depended on it. And maybe it wasn't her life, but it was going to get dark soon, and if she couldn't get Jules off the mountain, it was going to get cold and...she wasn't going to think about it. She waited a minute to let her panic recede before she went back to Jules. What had she just done?

She'd just sent a thirteen-year-old girl off by herself in an out-of-bounds area. What was she thinking?

Kylie took a deep breath and steeled herself. She needed to keep it together if she was going to keep Jules calm and that needed to be her first priority. She made her way through the deep snow and pulled some pine boughs off one of the trees and put them behind Jules, shifting her up so she sat on a makeshift blanket. Kylie didn't have much in the way of survival skills, but she did have some basic instincts and she had to keep Jules dry.

"How're you doing, kiddo? How's the pain?"

Jules's lip quivered. She'd been trying so hard to be brave, but it was easy to see the toll the situation was taking. "It hurts, Kylie. It hurts so much and I'm so sorry. I don't know what we were thinking. I know not to go out of bounds and—"

"It's okay, Jules." Kylie settled down next to her in the snow and held her hand. "It's all going to be okay."

As they settled in for what hopefully wouldn't be too long, Kylie hoped she wasn't lying.

HE WOULD HAVE LIKED to go for a quick ski to finish off the day, but by the time Malcolm got back to Stone Summit, it was just past three and the chairlifts would be taking up their final load before he'd have a chance to grab his gear. Instead, he took his time walking through the base of the hill where people milled about, meeting up with friends and finishing up their skiing for the day. There was a buzz in the air that made Malcolm smile; life was good and it was going to be even better once he found Kylie and put an end to the craziness between them.

And he would. He no longer had any doubt about it.

There was a commotion over at the ski patrol hut that caught Malcolm's attention. He didn't usually spend a lot of time over there—it was generally an area Seth handled—but they hadn't had any major injuries yet, so, curious, Malcolm headed over to check it out.

Seth was firing up a snowmobile and Piper Daniels was next to him with a backpack, attaching a stretcher to the back of another machine. A young girl he vaguely recognized sat on a bench crying while another one of the ski patrollers tried to console her.

Malcolm assessed the situation but still had no idea what was happening. He grabbed Seth's arm. "What's going on?"

Seth got up. "Tori came down the mountain alone, spouting off about how they'd gone out of bounds and Jules is hurt and—"

"Jules Martin?" Malcolm snapped to attention. "Beth's daughter?"

"That's the one."

"Out of bounds?"

Seth shook his head. "Hill policy is that we don't go out of bounds for recovery, but…"

"It's Jules." Malcolm shook his head. It was going to be a legal nightmare, and Malcolm already knew his lawyers were going to lose it if they sent employees out of bounds and something happened, but it wasn't up for negotiation. It was Jules.

"And Kylie."

Kylie. The name sent a shot of fear through him. "What?"

"Kylie's with her," Seth said distractedly. "I'm not sure of the whole story, but we need to get going. They're out past the glades, but Tori couldn't tell us the exact location. We don't have much time before dark."

He didn't think twice; there was no way it was going to happen any other way. "I'm coming."

"I can't let that happen." Seth held a gloved hand out. "You're not trained, Malcolm, and this is already a logistical nightmare. We need to move quickly."

"Kylie's out there." Just saying the words caused panic to rise up in him. "There's no way this is happening without me. Give me five minutes."

"Malcolm."

He didn't want to, but he pulled the boss card. "Don't forget who's in charge here, Seth. This does not happen without me."

For a moment, Seth looked as if he was going to object again, but then he closed his mouth and nodded. "Fine. But listen to me. You can come, but you cannot be in charge. I'm running this, and we'll do it my way."

Malcolm bit down an objection. "Fine."

"Okay, I'll send Piper out and I'll wait for you to grab your gear. Hurry."

It only took Malcolm a few minutes to change into his gear and grab his skis, which he strapped to the back of a snowmobile, and immediately they headed up the mountain. Malcolm's machine followed Seth's. He hated that he wasn't in control, especially because it was Kylie who was in danger. He longed to pull ahead and take the lead. The only thing that held him back was the fact that Malcolm had no details about where they were, and that made him even crazier. Every primal instinct in his body was on high alert, the need to protect his woman strong.

They rode hard and fast up the mountain, and soon they were approaching the trail that led to the little hut. Seth slowed and listened to the radio before he spoke into it. "Over here," he called out to Malcolm. "Piper found them. It's just a slight hike in from here. She parked her machine a little farther down, but if we put our skis on we can approach from here."

They moved quickly, putting the special covering skins on their skis that would allow them to hike through the snow faster. It had been awhile since Malcolm had been backcountry skiing, but it came back to him quickly and the men made good time pushing through the trees, over the out-of-bounds line and into the deeper snow. Every few steps, Seth spoke into the radio and changed course slightly. The sun was fading quickly and in the thicker trees, the muted sun cast shadows through the snow.

Then there they were. Malcolm picked up the pace and moved quickly. "Kylie!" He pushed harder up the hill, exerting more strength than he knew was smart. The moment he reached her, he pulled her into his arms and crushed her to him. "Thank God you're okay."

"Malcolm, what are you doing here? And of course I'm okay. I was just—"

Her words were lost as he crushed his lips to hers.

"Malcolm." Kylie pulled back. She smiled, but she also protested and pointed to the little audience they had. But he didn't care; he just wanted to pull her back to him and never let her go.

"I'm just so happy you're okay. I was so worried about you and when I heard you were up here, I…" He couldn't finish the sentence, because the thought of everything that actually did go through his mind when he heard they were staging a rescue mission that involved the woman he loved was too much to bear.

Kylie laughed. "I'm fine. Of course I am."

"Why would you go out of bounds, Kylie? Hell, even when we were kids and stupid we didn't—"

"It wasn't me." Kylie nodded toward Jules, who was being strapped into the sled by Piper and Seth. "I followed the girls. And it's a good thing I did. But I'm fine. Stop worrying."

"I'm not going to stop worrying until I get you safe and warm."

Malcolm stopped short of saying all the other things he wanted to do to her to keep her warm when he glanced over and saw Jules watching them. There'd be time for him to say everything he wanted to say to her when there weren't underage ears listening. "How are you doing, Jules?" He made his way over to the stretcher and checked on the girl, who was all strapped in and ready to go.

She nodded and tried to smile, but it wasn't hard to see the fear in the girl's eyes. "It'll be okay, Jules. I promise. Piper and Seth are the best. They'll take good care of you."

"We're ready to go," Seth said. He'd already pulled the skins off his skis and Piper had the handle of the stretcher around her waist.

"I'm going to get started," she said. "We need to get moving before it gets dark."

Malcolm looked back at Kylie, who was getting her skis ready. She was shivering; it was easy to see that she was exhausted. It would take her much too long to get through the difficult run and back to the lodge. He needed to get her warm, soon.

"Seth." He grabbed his buddy's arm before he could follow Piper. "Give me your radio." Malcolm was kicking himself for not taking a radio with him. He'd been so rushed, he hadn't thought to bring one, which was beyond stupid, but there was no time to worry about that now.

"Why? Aren't you guys coming?"

Malcolm glanced back behind him to Kylie, who was visibly struggling with her skis. She was too cold. "I've got to get her warm. Now. I'm going to take her to the hut. I'll make a fire and get her warm. As soon as we get out of the trees, I'll be able to get her on the sled and take her there. It'll be faster."

Seth nodded, handed over the radio and took off behind Piper.

Malcolm didn't waste any more time. He helped Kylie with her skis, gave her a pep talk about making the tight turns and soon they were out of the trees, on the snowmobile and headed toward the hut.

Chapter Fourteen

SHE HADN'T EXPECTED Malcolm to come and rescue her. Not really. But there was something about Malcolm: he was always there to take care of her and rescue her, no matter the situation. It had always been that way. She snuggled under the blankets he'd given her and watched him while he skillfully built the fire in the little hut. Their hut.

Almost a month ago, Malcolm's superhero tendencies drove Kylie crazy. It was different now. What was different about it? She pulled the quilt up around her chin. She was different. "Thank you," she said quietly.

He turned, a piece of wood in his hands. "For what?"

"For always being there, Malcolm. You just have a way of—"

"Kylie. I'll always be there for you. No matter what. Always."

She felt tears prick at her eyes and she didn't know whether it was the emotion of the day, what she'd just been through with Jules, or a buildup from the last few weeks, but she'd worked so hard to keep the tears at bay and she was no longer sure she could continue.

"Don't cry." Malcolm put the wood down and crawled over to her. He straddled her outspread legs, and took her face in his hands. "God, I thought I was going to lose you today."

She tried not to smile at the way he took it to extremes. "I wasn't in any danger of dying, Malcolm. It was just a hurt knee. And not even mine."

"No." He shook his head. "Do you have any idea what it's like to hear that the woman you love more than life itself is lost in the backcountry?"

She did smile then. "I can't say I do."

He took her chin in his hand and tilted it toward him. "It's terrible. And I never want to experience that again."

The look in Malcolm's eyes was so serious that the smile melted from her face. "You won't," she whispered. He was so close, she wanted to kiss him again. But despite the way he'd grabbed her and kissed her out on the hill, there was still too much between them just to fall into it again. They had things they needed to discuss. Kylie tilted her head to the side in an effort to put a little space between them. "We need to talk."

She tried not to notice the way his mouth set in a firm line when he crawled off her. "Yes, we do." He took his time feeding the fire before he returned to her spot on the floor under the blankets.

"I saw Marcus today," he said and she instantly tensed.

When he didn't immediately elaborate, she prompted, "And? How's Marcus?" It was a loaded question and they both knew it.

"We talked and he told—"

"Malcolm, please." She needed to stop him before it got out of hand again. She was so tired of dealing with whatever brotherly rivalry was going on between them. The only way to put a stop to it was to get tough and make her point clear. "This thing between us, it has nothing to do with Marcus. No, I shouldn't have kissed him at New Year's; that was my fault. I know it and I'm sorry. I was drinking and I was angry with you and…" She shook her head and looked away. "I can't keep having this same conversation. You need to accept once and for all that I don't love Marcus. I don't think I ever did. It was you, Malcolm. It was always you. Everything that happened at New Year's—well, nothing happened since and even though he thought for a minute that he wanted something to happen, he didn't. He never loved me either and it's—"

"I know."

"You need to let this jealousy of Marcus go. If we're ever—what?" His words caught up to her brain and she turned to look at him. "Wait? What? You know?"

Malcolm nodded, and his hand dug through the blankets to grab her hand. "I know, Kylie. He told me everything." Malcolm shrugged. "Well, he told me everything as far as he was concerned. I know that this has nothing to do with him. And I know that what you and I have is much stronger than anything you ever had with him."

His words hit her in her core, and a sense of relief washed through her. But there was still more, and they both knew it.

"So, are you ever going to tell me what is going on with you?" he asked outright. "Because I love you, Kylie, but I'm not a mind reader, and maybe I should have been paying more attention to you for the last few months and I know I'm not perfect." He ran a hand through his sexy, thick hair and the action made Kylie's heart clench. "Hell," he continued. "I'm far from perfect. But I'm really going to need your help here. What can I do to make this better?"

She took a deep breath and knew it was time to tell Malcolm everything. It was long past time. She took his hands in hers and squeezed them; she dropped a gentle kiss on them before she looked him in the eye. "I was scared," she said. "Really scared."

"Of what?"

Another deep breath and she was ready to tell him everything. Her fears of becoming her mother and losing her identity, the fear that she didn't even have an identity, her desire to be more and do more with her life—everything—and when she had finished, Malcolm closed his eyes and swallowed hard before he opened them again.

"Holy shit, Kylie."

She'd expected a lot of different responses from him, but that wasn't one of them. "Pardon?"

Malcolm laughed. "That's it?"

She sat back as if she'd been slapped. Was he really disregarding her feelings so easily?

He must have felt the tension because his laughter instantly dried up and he pulled her close, holding her tight so she couldn't get away. "No, no," he said. "That's not what I meant at all. I didn't mean it like, *that's it?* I meant it more like…ah fuck. Can I start over?"

She nodded.

"You have to understand, for the last few weeks I've been walking around not knowing what's going on with you and only had the most basic of clues. I mean, Archer isn't that great at reading women either." Kylie giggled a little. "So you have to know that I kept creating these worst-case scenarios in my head. And to hear you tell me what's really going on, well…babe." He pushed on her hands a little so she'd look up and meet his eyes. "It's such a relief because I can work with this. I can totally deal with this and help you with whatever it is you need from me, because, Kylie, you have to know, I do not want to be your parents either. I don't want to be my parents. I don't want to be anyone but us. I love you, Kylie. And I know I screwed up a little and forgot to tell you that every day and was a total ass on New Year's and there's no excuse for that, but you have to know that no matter what, I want what you want."

The whole time Malcolm spoke, Kylie's heart just got fuller

and fuller. She'd been such an idiot to shut him out the way she had, but she didn't regret the last few weeks alone. She couldn't because now more than ever, she knew what she wanted. When he had finished talking, she pulled her hands free from his and in a quick move, she freed herself from the nest of blankets and pushed him down so she hovered over top of him.

"Do you want to know what I want?"

His smile gave her all the answer she needed. "I hope to hell it's exactly what I want right now."

DESPITE EVERYTHING they'd been through, Malcolm knew that look in Kylie's eyes and knew exactly what she wanted and he was exactly the man to give it to her. He put one hand on the back of her head and pulled her mouth down to his while his other hand slid down to cup her ass. A groan escaped her lips and the sound was just about his undoing. "Fuck it." There was no way he could go slow with her, not tonight. Not after almost losing her, not after everything.

He wrapped his arms around her and flipped her over so he was on top of her and able to do whatever he wanted to her. And what he wanted to do was claim every part of her so there would never again be a mistake about where exactly she belonged. With him.

Kylie's eyes darkened, passion flaring to match his own.

"God, I want you," he growled. "Now."

Beneath him, she shimmied out of her leggings and he tugged her sweater over her head and unclipped her bra. Malcolm immediately dropped his mouth to her nipple and sucked the firm pebble into his mouth, eliciting another groan from her. While his mouth worked, alternating between each one of her luscious mounds, her hands slid down to his pants and past the waistband; it was his turn to groan.

"As much as I'm loving this, babe, I've had enough fooling around." He slipped his hand between her legs and found her deliciously wet and ready for him already. "I need you. Now."

He growled and nipped at her neck until she arched up into him and ground her pelvis against him in a way that he knew would be his undoing if he allowed it to continue.

"Enough." He took her hands and in one of his own, held her wrists over her head and pressed his hips into her, stilling the slow gyrating she was torturing him with.

The sound that came out of her mouth was somewhere between a groan and a squeal, so Malcolm turned his attention to her neck. He trailed kisses from the tender spot behind her earlobe, all the way down between her breasts, to her stomach where he twirled his tongue around her belly button, dipping it in momentarily, before he moved farther south.

He had to release her hands when he trailed his mouth to the apex of her thighs. She arched her back and laced her hands through Malcolm's hair, urging him on, but he didn't need any encouragement. With a hand on each thigh, he pushed her legs apart and used his tongue to taste her. She squirmed under his attentions, so he increased the pressure on her thighs and pinned her in place. He licked her seam slowly, torturously; she twisted beneath him.

"Malcolm, I…" Her hands fisted in his hair and she tugged him up until he was braced on his arms, his thick tip poised at her entrance.

Looking down at her, Malcolm was overwhelmed by the passion and love he felt for the woman beneath him. From the moment he'd laid eyes on her all those years ago, he'd known she was the one for him. There was no doubt: this woman belonged with him. No matter what it was she wanted, he knew without a doubt he'd go to the ends of the earth for her. As long as he had her, just like this, next to him, in his arms. Always.

"I love you, Kylie." He buried himself inside her with one strong thrust, never looking away from the love he saw reflected back in her eyes.

He cupped one hand around her cheek, the other one on her hip as she matched him thrust for thrust, until he felt the familiar tightening in her body that meant she was seconds away from coming undone beneath him. He crushed his mouth to hers, swallowing her moans of pleasure as she shattered around him. In that moment of their perfect union, seeing the love in Kylie's eyes, matching the love he felt for her, there was no doubt in Malcolm's mind that whatever was ahead of them, they'd be able to get through it. Together.

FOR KYLIE, there was nothing more amazing than making love to Malcolm. There never had been. She knew it from the first time they'd been together on the beach of the island of Eden; they fit together. Satisfied and content, she curled up in his arms, letting her head rest on his hard chest, and she knew that's exactly where she belonged. The doubts were gone. Nothing but certainty filled her, because being with him was different than it had ever been before. Something had shifted, and she couldn't quite put her finger on it, nor did she want to. She only wanted to absorb the feeling and let it fill her.

"You okay?" He kissed her forehead and stroked her hair off her face. She murmured an answer. "I'm going to take that as a yes."

"Take that as an...oh yes," she managed.

In response, he tightened his grip around her and pulled her even closer, if it was possible.

Last time they'd made love, in the very spot she now lay, it had been hard and passion fueled, and...not what they'd just had. She didn't want to overanalyze anything, but Kylie couldn't help it. Before she could stop herself, she asked, "What's different?"

Malcolm's hand stilled for a moment before he resumed the gentle stroke of her hair. "In what way?"

She shifted, so she was propped up on one elbow. "That was different." His face screwed up, so she quickly added, "Different in a very good way." She rested her hand on his chest, and moved her fingers distractedly.

His smile split his face and he reached up to cup her cheek. "God, Kylie. It was different because we're different. I love you. Hell, I think I've always loved you. But today, when I thought for even a moment that there was a chance I could lose you—"

"You weren't—"

He silenced her with a finger pressed to her lips. "Even for a moment," he repeated. "Just knowing you could be taken from me in an instant. I couldn't bear it, and I'm done with games. I'm done with this pretending we're not together when you and I both know that no matter how much distance you try to put between us for any reason, you cannot keep our hearts apart."

Her body responded to his words with a shiver and a twist low in her belly.

"We're meant to be together, Kylie." Unaware of the reaction his words had on her, he continued to talk. "For the last few weeks, we've been apart, and I thought it was going to kill me, but now I know the truth and so do you."

His finger trailed down her cheek and traced her lower lip. It may not have made much sense to anyone else, but it didn't have to. Kylie knew exactly what he was talking about. She'd been a fool to put space between them when it was so clear there was nowhere else she'd rather be than in his arms.

Except for one thing.

She'd forgotten all about nursing school and the opportunity she had. Being stuck with Jules in the woods, unable to do anything more than offer her encouragement and support, she'd felt totally helpless. If she'd been trained, maybe she could have done more to help the girl.

"Kylie?"

She looked down at Malcolm, who watched her as if she might break any moment. Her eyes filled with tears because she knew he was right. They couldn't be apart. Their hearts were meant to be together. Even when she'd tried to put space between them, it hadn't worked because it could never work. She loved him too much for it to be any other way. For the first time, she realized exactly why her mother had stayed with her dad all those years. She'd loved him too much to do anything else but stand by him. She'd stepped back into the shadows and let him shine out of love.

Looking at the man whom she loved more than anything else, Kylie knew it would physically break her to lose him, but what would it do to her if she let her dream go? Her stomach twisted at the thought of what she knew she had to do.

"Kylie? Look at me." She blinked hard and forced a smile she didn't feel to her face. "You feel the same, right?"

"You have to ask?"

"Not really, but I saw that look on your face, and I'm not going to take any chances again. What's going on?"

She shook her head and swallowed hard. "Nothing," she lied. "I'm just happy we've figured it all out and—"

"To hell with that." He slid out from under her so abruptly, she almost lost her balance. Catching herself, she scooted over and wrapped a blanket around her shoulders. "You don't think this," he gestured between them, "fixes everything? Because we still have a lot to talk about, and I'm not leaving here until we figure it out once and for all."

HE COULD SEE what was happening and Malcolm would be dammed if he was going to let her avoid this conversation. It needed to be done. Hell, they should have talked about all this stuff a long time ago. A very long time ago. He may have been a total idiot before, too wrapped up in the ski hill to see what was going on with Kylie, but the last few weeks had opened his eyes. As had a few pointed conversations with his friends.

He'd wasted too much time already thinking that Marcus was the root of their troubles. Now he knew different. A conversation they'd only briefly had the last time they were at the cabin kept haunting him.

"What is it you want, Kylie?"

The look on her face told him he'd totally caught her off guard. "Pardon?"

"I mean it. What do you want?" She opened her mouth to answer, and he held up a finger. "I mean, besides me."

"I'm confused." She shook her head and looked as if she might cry. "I thought…us…I guess I…"

The blanket he was holding fell away as he put his hands on her knees and squeezed. "I'm doing this wrong. I'm sorry. Look at me." She did. "I love you, Kylie Wilson, and no matter what, I'm going to be with you. On one condition." Her eyes widened in question, but he still didn't give her a chance to protest or ask questions. "I need you to have everything you want, and that includes following your dreams, whatever they are."

Tears pooled in her eyes.

"Malcolm, I—"

"I know you have them and I know I've been a fool and totally wrapped up in my own stuff for far too long. But that changes, now. I remember when we were kids, you said you wanted to be a nurse." Something flashed in her eyes. "Do you still want that?"

He knew he'd hit on something, because she grew very still

and one tear slipped down her cheek. He reached up and used his thumb to wipe it away. He couldn't bear to see her cry, particularly if he was, even in some small way, responsible for those tears. "Talk to me, Kylie."

She shook her head. "I'm so sorry, Malcolm."

"No. Don't be sorry for anything."

"But I am. I want to be with you more than anything else in the world."

"I know that." He kept his voice soft, but firm; he needed her to admit what she really wanted, and he was not going to let her leave until he'd heard every one of her dreams and desires. Malcolm knew she had them, and it was long past time for her to share those with him. "What else do you want?"

She didn't protest, or try to deflect the question. Instead, she looked down and took a deep breath. When she looked up, tears streamed down her face. There was no way he could wipe them all away and he didn't want to distract her, when she looked as if she was finally ready to talk. It pained him to do so, but he waited.

Finally, her voice cracking, she spoke. "I want a career. I want to have something of my own that I can be proud of and makes me whole. Something that makes a difference. I want to…no. I'm going to be a nurse."

He knew it. His heart soared, but her next words sent it crashing.

"I leave in a few weeks."

FINALLY SAYING the words out loud, Kylie knew there was no doubt: she would take the spot in school, even if it meant that her heart would fracture into a million pieces. There was no way she could be with Malcolm, knowing it was because of him that she gave up her dream. It wasn't fair to him, and she was smart enough to know that she was nothing like her mother. She couldn't stand by and let her man shine, knowing she'd given up on herself in order to do so.

Telling Malcolm and saying the words out loud after so long lifted a weight from her, but if finally saying what she'd been thinking was supposed to be so freeing, why did she feel so terrible? She couldn't meet his eyes.

"You leave in a few weeks?"

She nodded but didn't look up. "I was accepted into an accelerated program, but it doesn't leave me much time for—"

"That's awesome!"

"I know it's—what?" She lifted her gaze to see that Malcolm had sat up on his knees. The blanket had slid even further; his arms were outstretched and he had a huge grin on his face. If she hadn't been so distracted by their conversation, she might have been even more distracted by his nakedness. "What did you say?"

He leaned forward and wrapped her in a bear hug. "I'm so proud of you, Kylie. That's fantastic."

"It is?" Didn't he understand that going to school meant she'd be leaving and they couldn't be together? Did he not catch that part? "What part of me going away is fantastic?"

He kissed her on the top of her head and pulled back so she could see his face, which was animated and clearly excited. "The part where you'll be following your dream." He looked at her as if she had three heads. "What's not fantastic about that?"

All the emotions inside her swirled together so quickly, Kylie struggled to sort everything out. He was excited she was going? Did he not understand what it meant? She had to make him understand.

"Malcolm, the school is in Vancouver." She spoke slowly, and watched his face for the moment when he would recognize what it all really meant. "It's a two-year program. I have to move."

He nodded while she spoke, which only infuriated her. How could he not understand?

"Malcolm." Kylie struggled to keep her voice level. Was he really going to make her say it out loud? That she chose her dream over him? That despite how it broke her heart, she knew she had to follow her dream? "Stone Summit is here. This is where you live."

"I'm aware of where I live, Kylie."

Frustration built inside her until she thought she would scream. She jerked her hands away from him and jumped to her feet, taking the blanket with her. "You don't get it. I have to move away and that means this…" she waved one hand between them, "us…we can't happen."

"Why not?" He stood and took a step toward her.

"Because I'll be gone." She knew she was yelling, but she couldn't stop herself. It hurt too much to know she'd be walking away from him, and he was definitely not making it any easier. "It's not fair to you to ask you to—"

"To what?" Malcolm stood inches from her and stared down at her. "You're not asking me to do anything. I just finished telling you I loved you, Kylie, and I meant it. Whatever you want, it's what I want. Do you not know that by now? We'll make it work."

Her lower lip trembled and she bit down to keep from crying. "But it's two years."

"I want to spend a lifetime with you." He tilted her chin up so she looked at him. The love in his eyes was her undoing and the tears started fresh. "Two years is nothing. There are cars and airplanes and…nothing will keep me away from you, babe. Nothing."

Hearing the words from his mouth, Kylie somehow believed them. It wouldn't be easy. It would be far from easy.

But he loved her. And God help her, she loved him so much it hurt.

"Do you believe me?"

She nodded.

"Good." He slid his hands under the blanket she still clutched to herself, and for the first time, she realized he didn't have one of his own. "Because we'll make it work. I'm not letting you go. Not for anything."

She believed him; they would make it work. They had to because she knew she wasn't ever going to let him go either.

As Malcolm pulled her naked body to his own, pressing her up against his length, she dropped her own blanket and let the heat of him warm her as everything finally became clear.

She'd almost lost him because of her doubts. But never again. She could have it all. Kylie reached up and pulled his mouth to hers. As she lost herself in the taste of the man she loved, she knew the truth: she already had it all.

Epilogue

THE DAYS HAD FLOWN by in a whirlwind of activity as Kylie made the final preparations for her move to Vancouver. She couldn't believe she'd almost given up on such an opportunity. Just thinking of the way she'd behaved with Malcolm still made Kylie shake her head.

Not that any of that mattered anymore. She was all packed up, and with his support and more love than she ever thought possible, she was ready to make the move.

Almost.

First she needed to finish saying goodbye to her best friend.

"This day has come too fast," Cynthia moaned as she hugged her again.

Kylie laughed, even though she agreed. If she didn't laugh, she would cry. And she wasn't upset. She really wasn't. "I know," she said. "But it's not permanent. I'll be back a lot. And it's only for two years and then it will be like I never left."

Cynthia tipped her head and gave her a look. "I don't know about that, but I am happy for you," she added. "I really am."

"Thank you." She squeezed her friend again. "And I'm

only a phone call away if you need to talk or if you need to tell me anything…" she winked at her friend. "Like about a guy maybe…"

Cynthia waved her hand in dismissal. "I doubt that. Not in this town."

"You never know." She wiggled her eyebrows, but Kylie knew enough not to push too hard. "Okay." She took a deep breath. "I really do have to go." She gave her friend one last hug and then before either of them could cry, slipped out the door and into the snow.

AS CYNTHIA GILES stood at the door of her shop and watched her best friend run through the snow that had just started to fall. The street lights had just come on, lighting up Main Street and the falling snow so it looked like a snow globe.

She'd done her best to ignore the calendar this year, but despite her efforts, Valentine's Day had come way too quickly. Never mind everything else the stupid commercial holiday meant, as if to add insult to injury this year, it also meant the day to say goodbye to her best friend was that much closer. Ever since Kylie announced she was going to nursing school, things had been crazy. Cynthia'd done her duty as a best friend and helped her pack and take care of the details. Of course they'd spent some time together, but it was still hard knowing she wouldn't be right around the corner in a few days. Kylie would be going next week to find an apartment in Vancouver, and as much as Cynthia wanted to be the one to go with her and get her set up, it would be Malcolm going with her.

Of course it would. Because Malcolm was her boyfriend and if Cynthia had a boyfriend, she might know that same kind of love and dedication. But she didn't.

She smacked the Mylar heart balloon that was tied next to

the register so it bounced wildly around the display she'd had Colton, her part-time kid, set up last week. She wouldn't have put up a display at all since she hated the dumb holiday, but it was commercial and she was in the business of selling things, so it was kind of required. But it didn't mean she had to like it.

She glanced at the clock over the door. It was already after six. She closed up in less then an hour and as far as she was concerned, if people hadn't bought their loved ones anything by now, they didn't deserve to have their loved ones. Cynthia picked up a white stuffed bear holding a heart and squeezed it. Not that a stupid stuffed animal would be a good gift for anyone over fourteen. Which was probably the last time she got a Valentine's Day gift. Not that she was bitter about it. Nope. Not her.

"Stupid bear." She wound up and threw the bear as hard as she could at the door, right as the bells chimed.

"Wow." Seth McBride walked into the store and easily caught the bear before it hit him in the chest. "And I didn't get you anything."

To her annoyance, a blush rose up her neck and heated her face. It was an annoying trait that as a redhead she blushed easy and hard. It was extra annoying that it always seemed to happen around Seth. At least, it'd been happening since New Year's, and they…no. She needed to distract herself.

"Don't tell me." Cynthia put as much attitude in her voice as she could. She leaned up against the counter and crossed her arms over her chest. "You have a date with some ski bunny whose name you can barely remember and you thought that since it's Valentine's Day, you would seal the deal with a box of overpriced waxy chocolates."

The smile slipped from his face, and for a second, Cynthia felt guilty for being such a bitch. She couldn't help it; there was something about Seth and his playboy ways that got her riled up.

Especially because they weren't directed at her. She pushed the thought down, unwilling to entertain it for even a second.

"If you must know," he took a step closer to her, "I am not here for chocolates."

His eyes flicked to the left, where the personal care aisles were. No way. If Seth McBride was seriously going to buy condoms from her, she was going to die on the spot. Nothing could be more mortifying.

She swallowed hard, determined not to let him see that he affected her in any way. "Then what are you here for? I'm about to close up."

He raised an eyebrow. "You don't close for another forty minutes."

"Did it occur to you that I might be closing down early tonight because I have a date?"

Where had that lie come from? Sometimes she scared herself with her ability to dig holes she couldn't get out of.

"You have a date?"

Did he look jealous? Maybe. There might have been a bit of jealousy. Or maybe it was just annoyance.

"Well, it is Valentine's Day. Don't you?"

She could have smacked herself when he walked past her with a shake of his head. "Not this year."

It's not that she was normally a liar, or that she ever made a practice of making up fake dates, but for some reason she wished she could explain, she felt the overwhelming need for Seth to think she wasn't going to be sitting alone with a bottle of wine and no one to share it with on Valentine's Day except for her sick mom, who at this time of night should be doped up on pain meds and fast asleep for the evening. It was sad. Worse than sad—it was pathetic, and she definitely didn't want Seth to know it. Even if that's more or less what he'd just told her. Well, all except for the sitting alone with a bottle of wine part.

"So what are you looking for tonight?" She followed him

through the store with her eyes. He stopped by the personal aisle where they kept the condoms, and as if he knew it was torturing her—which he probably did know—he turned and gave her one of his ridiculously killer smiles.

"It's too bad you have a date," he said. "I was going to offer to show you."

"Show me what?"

The way he looked at her, Cynthia had a feeling she might regret asking the question. Or perhaps the opposite was true, and she would be very thankful she asked. Either way, it wasn't as if she had much to lose.

Seth kept walking, moving to the pet aisle at the back of the store. "I had a visitor today." He picked up a large bag of dog kibble and heaved it easily to his shoulder. "A beautiful husky showed up at the hill, and found her way into the maintenance shack where we kept the sleds."

"How do you know it's a her?" Cynthia cleared a space on the counter for his purchases.

He grinned again, and God help her, it made her stomach flip in ways it shouldn't. "Because a few hours ago, she welcomed a few more little guests."

"What? Guests? Oh…" Cynthia's hand flew to her mouth as she realized what Seth was saying. "You mean, puppies?"

He nodded, obviously excited to share the news with her. "Three of them. I gave her some old blankets and a space heater, and as soon as I got them set up, I came to get supplies for the little guys."

"You do know that puppies don't eat kibble, right?"

He narrowed his eyes at her joke, but laughed with her. "Yeah, yeah. I know. But the mama's gonna be hungry and since I have no idea where she belongs, I thought I'd help her out."

Seriously? What was it about the man that just kept getting more and more attractive? She really needed to focus on everything else about him that she didn't like. Like the fact that he spent all his time outdoors. She hated that. And...

"So do you want to come see them?"

Her mental list evaporated with the lure of puppies. "Of course. Just let me lock up."

Seth paid for the food and pulled it off the counter. As soon as she was done ringing him up, she locked up the till. She'd worry about the cash-out later. It's not as if she had anyone to answer to, anyway.

Either way, it didn't matter and it gave her a lot more freedom. "Just let me grab my purse."

Seth was waiting for her by the door when she was ready. He stopped her with a gentle touch to her elbow. "I thought you had a date tonight?"

They locked eyes, each challenging the other. He knew damn well she didn't have a date. She hadn't had a date in weeks. Six, to be exact. Not since New Year's Eve. And calling a totally unplanned and irresponsible hookup a date was a stretch by any standards. And a few weeks later when it happened again—well, that couldn't be considered a date because again, they hadn't meant to bump into each other at the Paw and have too many drinks, and they certainly hadn't meant to go back to her place and...

"No." She flicked off the light. "I mean, I do...I did...but, hey, we should go and make sure the puppies are okay." She knew she sounded like an idiot, and the last thing she wanted was to be affected by him in any way.

Grateful for the distraction, she followed him out and turned to lock the door behind them. When she turned around, he stood so close she almost bumped up against him. She caught herself by putting a hand on his chest and her whole body thrilled at the touch.

He held her gaze. "I'm glad."

Too late. She was definitely affected by him and that was

really too bad, because nothing could ever happen between them. Not again.

———

What happened between Cynthia and Seth? Will it happen again? They say opposites attract...but will they combust? Find out in Summit of Seduction! You can read an exclusive excerpt right after this——

>

And if you want even more romance...click HERE for an exclusive FREE novella that isn't available anywhere else!

Summit of Seduction

There were a million other places Cynthia Giles should be. Well, maybe not a million. But there were definitely a few other places she could think of that would be more appropriate for her to be on Valentine's Day night besides riding in a pickup truck, only a bump and jostle away from bouncing into Seth McBride, who sat only inches away from her. Inches.

Too close.

Way too close. Especially considering every nerve in her body was totally aware of his proximity and was going completely haywire because of it. Sure, she'd been in close spaces with Seth before. Very close. But that was different. Her body should not be betraying her with its obvious and totally uncontrollable attraction to him. Even if he was incredibly handsome in that rugged mountain man, outdoorsy way. If that was your kind of thing. And it was most certainly not her kind of thing. At least it hadn't been.

Cynthia risked a glance over at him. One hand rested casually on the steering wheel as he navigated the truck through the snowy roads as if he'd done it a thousand times, which he probably had. A lock of his hair flopped over his eye. He swiped it away, and in doing so, caught her looking at him.

"If you want me to drop you somewhere, I can," he said. "You don't have to come with me."

It was the second time he'd tested her, trying to give her an out. From the moment he'd set foot in her shop, the Store Room, he'd been testing her, almost as if he'd been trying to get her to admit something she wouldn't. But what? It was Valentine's Day. It was bad enough that she didn't have a date. She didn't have to admit it to him. Not Seth McBride. Not after what they'd….

"No," she said quickly, and returned her gaze straight ahead out the windshield to the snow that started to come down harder. "I told you I'd come to check on the puppies, and I will."

Less than an hour ago, he'd come into her store to buy dog kibble for a stray husky who'd found her way into the maintenance shed at Stone Summit, the local ski hill where he was general manager, and had a litter of puppies. Or at least that was the story he told her. Not that he had any reason to lie. Why would he?

To get her to spend Valentine's Day with him, a little voice in the back of her head said.

She quickly dismissed it. Seth wasn't the type of guy to go to such lengths to get a girl to spend time with him. Hell, he wasn't the type of guy to go to any lengths. He was the type of guy who worked his way through women like consumables. It was well known around town that Seth McBride didn't *do* relationships. He did one-night stands and casual flings, but that was it. She herself had known it for years; even if she did have a momentary lapse of judgment—twice—and thought maybe, just maybe it could be different with her…that moment was over.

"If you insist." There was a hint of humor in his voice and she whipped around in her seat.

"I don't insist." How the hell did he do that? Turn it into her idea? It was Seth who had walked into her store and told her about the puppies. It was Seth who asked her if she wanted to come see them. "You're the one who…" She trailed off at his grin. He was trying to get her riled up. And it worked.

Cynthia crossed her arms and faced forward again. "Why do you do that?"

"What?"

"Like to get me worked up."

"Because you're incredibly sexy when you're mad." Seth spoke the words so simply it took her off guard. She risked another glance at him but he was focused on driving as he turned down the short road that led to Stone Summit, the newly reopened ski hill that Malcolm Stone owned and Seth managed. A job that was set to become even busier now that Malcolm's girlfriend, Cynthia's best friend, Kylie Wilson, was getting ready to leave town to go to school in Vancouver. Malcolm planned to split his time between Vancouver and the ski hill, which would leave Seth primarily in charge. *A role that would no doubt go to his head even more*, Cynthia thought with a sniff.

She couldn't explain why she was so antagonistic toward the man. Okay, she could. She just didn't want to. It was a proven fact that Seth was a womanizer and she hated herself for her moment of weakness and falling for his charms. Not once, but twice. She was not that girl. Sure, Cynthia liked to have a good time. She liked to enjoy herself and no one appreciated a party more than she did. But after a failed attempt at a relationship with Jax Carver, the head chef at the Springs, she'd sworn off men. Or more specifically, men who weren't interested in something serious. And it was clear Seth wasn't interested. But he didn't have to be such an ass about it.

"I'm sorry," Seth said, taking her off guard.

For a second, she thought maybe he was finally going to apologize for the way he'd gotten what he wanted from her and then quickly moved on to the next woman in line. She raised her eyebrow and waited for him to say more.

"I didn't mean to make you mad." He grinned and she hated the way her body responded to him while at the same time she wanted to smack the smile off his face.

She shook her head. Only a few weeks ago, Cynthia had thought things could be different between them, that maybe the connection they shared physically was enough to actually turn into something more. Because, damn, even if she didn't want to admit it, there was definitely a physical connection between them. She'd actually been naive enough to think that maybe the right guy for her had been under her nose all along, disguised as Seth McBride. But then she'd discovered his true colors when she caught him having dinner at the Stillwater Grill with some other woman. She hadn't even seen her face, nor had she bothered to confront him about it. Why would she? It's not as if they were dating. Besides, she'd known that was how Seth was right from the start. It shouldn't have come as a surprise. Her anger was her shield, and she'd carry it as long as it took for her to forget the way his touch made her feel, the way his kiss made her come alive.

"Hey." Seth grabbed her arm, forcing her to turn and face him. "I *am* sorry, Cyn. Really."

The light was too dark for her to read his eyes to see whether he was being sincere, but there was something in his voice that she believed and she let some of her hostility melt away. After all, even if there was nothing between them, spending the night visiting newborn puppies certainly beat the alternative, which was sitting home alone and drinking a bottle of wine by herself on Valentine's Day. And he did say she looked sexy. She forced herself not to smile.

"How many puppies did you say there were?"

He grinned; his teeth flashed in the dim light of the truck. "Three."

She nodded. "Right."

Seth looked at her a moment longer and held her eyes for just a fraction of a second before he turned back to the road. She turned her head again and mentally chastised herself. *Get it together, Cynthia. He's just a guy. Just a guy.*

She could tell herself that all she wanted, but it was a lie and she damn well knew it. Seth McBride was more than a guy.

"Here we are."

Cynthia snapped to attention as Seth pulled up next to the steel building that she knew housed the snow groomers and snowmobiles for the ski hill. She'd never actually been in the maintenance shed—why would she? But she'd spent enough time at Stone Summit to know most of the buildings.

After Seth hopped out of the truck, she waited for a moment to see whether he'd come around and open her door. He didn't. Not that she expected him to. It's not as though they were on a date or anything. *Still*. With a sigh, Cynthia opened the door and turned to slide out into the chilly night.

"Here." To her surprise, Seth held his hand out for her. "Let me help you."

It took her a second to realize what he was offering. She looked at his hand and then back at him. "I got it." With a less than glamorous move, Cynthia hopped down from the cab of the truck. When she saw the look on his face, she instantly regretted not accepting his help. Before she could say or do anything, he turned away and went to retrieve the bag of kibble from the back.

"They're right in here." Seth gestured with his head and Cynthia followed as he led the way into the shed.

They dodged and weaved their way past equipment and

workbenches; the smell of oil and something else, something distinctly male, hung in the air. She'd never been in such a space before. It felt oddly as if she were trespassing into some other world. Seth's world. She watched him, matching his steps, being sure to avoid the bits of machinery that stuck out until they reached the far corner of the shed.

"You put her way in the back?"

Seth shrugged casually. "Don't blame me." He gave her that sly smile again. "She chose the spot. I just went with it. Stubborn female and all that." He winked and looked away.

Cynthia shook her head and looked around him. "Is that her, over there?"

"Just in the corner. Maybe be careful before you get too close to her pups." He put a hand on her arm to still her. Cynthia froze, but not because of the action. More from the electricity that flew through her from one simple touch. Even through her winter jacket, his touch had a powerful effect on her. She had to turn away, unable to look him in the eye. "I don't know how she'll react, Cyn. I wouldn't want you to—"

"What?"

When he didn't answer, she turned and their eyes locked. For a moment, she thought she saw something else in his dark brown eyes, but then he blinked and the moment was gone. "I don't know the dog," he said quickly. "And you never know how a new mom will react. Let alone a stray. Just be careful."

She slipped past him and moved toward the box in the corner. "Don't worry, I'll—" Her words dropped away when she saw the beautiful husky with three impossibly tiny little puppies tucked up next to her. The dog lifted her head and looked at her with big, sorrowful eyes. Cynthia dropped to her knees on the concrete and reached her hand out to the dog, who sniffed it once before she licked it and tilted her head into Cynthia's hand to be stroked. Of course, Cynthia obliged.

"She likes you." Seth was next to her, on his knees on the

concrete and for once, Cynthia's stomach didn't flip or react at his proximity. Instead, all her energy was focused on the dog.

"What's her name?"

"I told you, she's a stray. She wandered in here earlier tonight and—"

"I know, but she needs a name. She's a mama now. It seems wrong to keep calling her *the dog*." Cynthia scratched the dog's ears for another second before the dog bent her head to attend to her puppies. She licked them all in turn and nuzzled them closer to her belly. "She's beautiful and look how much she loves her babies." Cynthia's heart swelled. She'd always had a soft spot when it came to animals, although somehow she'd never had a pet of her own. When she was younger, her mother was so busy working that she refused to take on the responsibility of another life; even though Cynthia would beg her and try to convince her that she'd do all the work, it hadn't worked. As she got older, it was easy to see that her mother might have been right. Besides, she was too busy being a teenager and getting into trouble; a pet was the last thing from her mind. By the time she was old enough to really think about it again, her mother had been diagnosed with breast cancer and she'd had her hands full of taking care of her and the store.

"What are you thinking?"

Cynthia's smile was sad, but she answered Seth honestly. "I was just thinking how much I missed by never having a pet."

"You've never had a dog?"

She shook her head.

"Or a cat?"

She shook her head again.

"Well then, I think you should name her."

She turned her head to see Seth only inches away from her. He was close enough to kiss and for a moment she let herself entertain the idea. But only for a moment. She looked back at the dog. "The fact that I've never had a pet hardly makes me qualified to name her."

"It makes you perfectly qualified." His voice was low and sexy and she knew without looking that he stared at her. With renewed determination, she kept her gaze fixed on the dog.

"Okay…" She pondered her options but there was only one that spoke to her. "Nala."

"Nala?"

"It means loved." Cynthia reached out and stroked the dog's soft fur. "And I think she definitely loves and is loved." The puppies wriggled and made soft mewling sounds until Nala tended to them and nudged them gently with her muzzle. "Yes." Unbidden tears pricked at her eyes and she blinked hastily to keep them at bay.

Silently, Seth moved around behind her and wrapped his arm around her. She didn't slide away the way she should have and when he pulled her in to his chest, instead of stopping him, she leaned into his solid muscle. He was strong and warm and smelled of fresh cut wood and something else that was uniquely Seth. She closed her eyes against the unexpected emotion the dog and her puppies brought on and let herself have the moment in Seth's arm. Because that's all it would be.

Just a moment.

Damn.

She felt good in his arms.

He had no claim on her, no reason to reach out and hold her. In fact, Seth had half-expected Cynthia to pull away and put that ever present distance between them again. But the moment he saw the tears in her eyes, he'd acted totally on instinct. There was no way he was going to sit by and watch her get emotional. Not that it meant anything, he told himself. He would have done the same for any woman. He simply could not handle it when women cried or got upset.

Especially Cynthia.

He shut down the thought. Besides a few hookups—a few hookups that had been nothing short of freaking amazing— they had nothing. They were friends. And even then, they hardly seemed like friends these days. For a while, Seth thought that maybe there could be something between the two of them. He'd never felt that way about another woman before. After all, his entire MO was to have fun and get out before it got serious. Growing up with just his dad and his string of girl- friends after his mom died, it was easy for him to swear off serious relationships.

Things with Cynthia felt different, but then, just when he started to consider something more than just a casual fling, she pulled away. He couldn't explain it, but she stopped answering his calls, and made a point to ignore him when they ran into each other. He'd never pretended to understand women, but Cynthia was in a class of confusing all on her own.

It didn't matter anyway, because really, they had nothing in common besides a few joint friends. Besides, she'd made it clear that she didn't want anything further to do with him. He should have been smart enough to leave her alone.

But he couldn't.

Something about the damn woman kept him coming back. Had him seeking her out. Just the way he had earlier tonight. It was Valentine's Day. She should have had a date and even though she said she did, he knew she didn't. Not that he could understand it. With her long, lean body with curves in all the right places, and the fiery red hair that he knew for damn sure was natural, the woman was smoking hot. There was no reason she shouldn't have had a date.

Unless...

No. He wasn't going to put any more thought into it. For the moment, she was in his arms and she felt damn good. That was good enough for him.

"What's wrong?" He whispered into her ear, close enough to kiss her earlobe. An urge he fought. "Are you okay?"

She nodded against his chest. "I'm fine. I just…I don't know. It's just so sweet watching her. The immediate love and instinct she has for her babies." She turned in his arms so their noses almost touched. He could feel her soft breath on his face. "Do you think every mom feels that way?"

Again, he fought the urge to kiss her, knowing she'd just pull away and the moment would be lost. "I do. I've seen a lot of animals with their babies, and I've yet to see any mother who didn't react just the way Nala has."

Her smile was gorgeous and even in the dim maintenance shed, it lit up her face. "Nala," she repeated. "Do you like the name?"

"It's perfect."

Their eyes locked and Seth moved his hand up her back and brushed her hair off the back of her neck. Forget every reason he shouldn't. No matter what it was Cynthia thought she was running from, it felt right being with her. He closed the slight gap between them and brushed her lips with his. They were soft and slightly chilled from the cool air, but after a moment she opened to him in a soft, slow kiss. His body responded at once with the promise of what was to come. Gently, he pulled her to her feet without leaving her mouth and pulled her even closer until their bodies were pressed together.

Just as he began to think it might be a good Valentine's Day after all, Cynthia stepped back and broke their kiss.

Damn her pushing him away again.

"Cynthia, why are you—"

"I don't think…No." Her hand went to her mouth and she shook her head. "I should probably get going."

"You don't have to go." He reached for her again. "We have such a good time together."

Something flashed across her face and then the confusion

was gone, replaced by a hardness as she closed herself off again. "We did," she said. "Once."

"Twice."

Her eyes flashed and she took a deep breath. "I have...I have a date."

He opened his mouth to call her bluff. When he'd walked into the Store Room to pick up the bag of kibble, she'd said something about a date for Valentine's Day but he hadn't believed her. Or had he just not wanted to believe her?

"With who?" He hated that he probably came off as a jealous boyfriend; that wasn't his style. Not even a little. He didn't care. Except when it came to the woman in front of him, he did. And it made him crazy.

She looked at him then and stared right into his soul with those striking jade green eyes. "It's none of your business, Seth McBride."

You had your chance. She didn't say it, but she might as well have for the way she looked at him and crossed her arms over her chest, shutting him out.

Seth shook his head, ran a hand through his hair and gave her his best shit-eating grin. "Well, I wouldn't want you to be late for Mr. Wonderful." It was easier to be an ass than try to get to the bottom of whatever it was that was going on with her. Besides, if she didn't want him, plenty of women would.

He stalked off through the shed, not waiting for her to follow but knowing she would.

Read the rest of Summit of Seduction **NOW!**

About the Author

Elena Aitken is a USA Today Bestselling Author of more than forty romance and women's fiction novels. The mother of 'grown up' twins, Elena now lives with her very own mountain man in the heart of the very mountains she writes about. She can often be found with her toes in the lake and a glass of wine in her hand, dreaming up her next book and working on her own happily ever after.

To learn more about Elena:
www.elenaaitken.com
elena@elenaaitken.com